PRAISE FOR *FLUNKED*

"Another winner from Jen Calonita. Charming fairy-tale fun."

—Sarah Mlynowski, author of the *New York Times* bestselling Whatever After series

"Fairy Tale Reform School is spell-binding and wickedly clever. Gilly is smart, spunky, and a hilarious narrator, and I cannot wait to read about her next adventure!"

—Leslie Margolis, author of the Annabelle Unleashed novels and the Maggie Brooklyn mysteries

"Fairy Tale Reform School is a fresh and funny take on the enchanted world. (And who hasn't always wanted to know what happened to Cinderella's stepmother?)"

—Julia DeVillers, author of the Trading Faces identical twin series and *Emma Emmets, Playground Matchmaker*

"This clever novel and its smart, endearing cast of characters will have readers enchanted and eager for the implied sequel(s)."

—Bulletin of the Center for Children's Books

"Gilly's plucky spirit and determination to oust the culprit will make *Flunked* a popular choice for tweens."

—School Library Journal

"There's much to amuse and entertain fans of classic tales with a twist."

—Booklist

More Praise for Jen Calonita

"A must-read, full of scandals, sisterhood, southern charm and secrets!"

—Sara Shepard, #1 bestselling author of the Pretty Little Liars series on Belles

"This is a surefire hit for teens who like stories about friendship, romance, and mean girls getting a taste of their own medicine. The second in a series, this book can be read alone but would be best enjoyed in order."

—VOYA on Belles

FAIRY TALE REFORM SCHOOL

FLUNKED

JEN CALONITA

Cover and internal design ©2015 by Sourcebooks, Inc.
Cover design by Regina Flath
Cover image by Mike Heath/Shannon Associates

Published by Sourcebooks Jabberwocky, an imprint of Sourcebooks, Inc.
P.O. Box 4410, Naperville, Illinois 60567-4410
(630) 961-3900
Fax: (630) 961-2168
www.sourcebooks.com

The Library of Congress has cataloged the hardcover edition as follows:

Calonita, Jen.
Flunked / Jen Calonita.
pages cm. -- (Fairy Tale Reform School)
Summary: When petty thief Gilly, who lives with five younger brothers and sisters in a run-down boot, gets caught stealing, she is sentenced to Fairy Tale Reform School, where all of the teachers are former villains, including the Big Bad Wolf, the Evil Queen, and Cinderella's Wicked Stepmother.
(13 : alk. paper) [1. Fairy tales--Fiction. 2. Characters in literature--Fiction. 3. Good and evil--Fiction. 4. Reformatories--Fiction. 5. Schools--Fiction.] I. Title.
PZ7.C1364Gr 2013
[Fic]--dc23

2014039606

Source of Production: Versa Press, East Peoria, Illinois, USA
Date of Production: December 2015
Run Number: 5005339

Printed and bound in the United States of America.
VP 10 9 8 7 6 5 4 3 2

For Tyler and Dylan, who have been waiting for me to write something they could read "forever!"

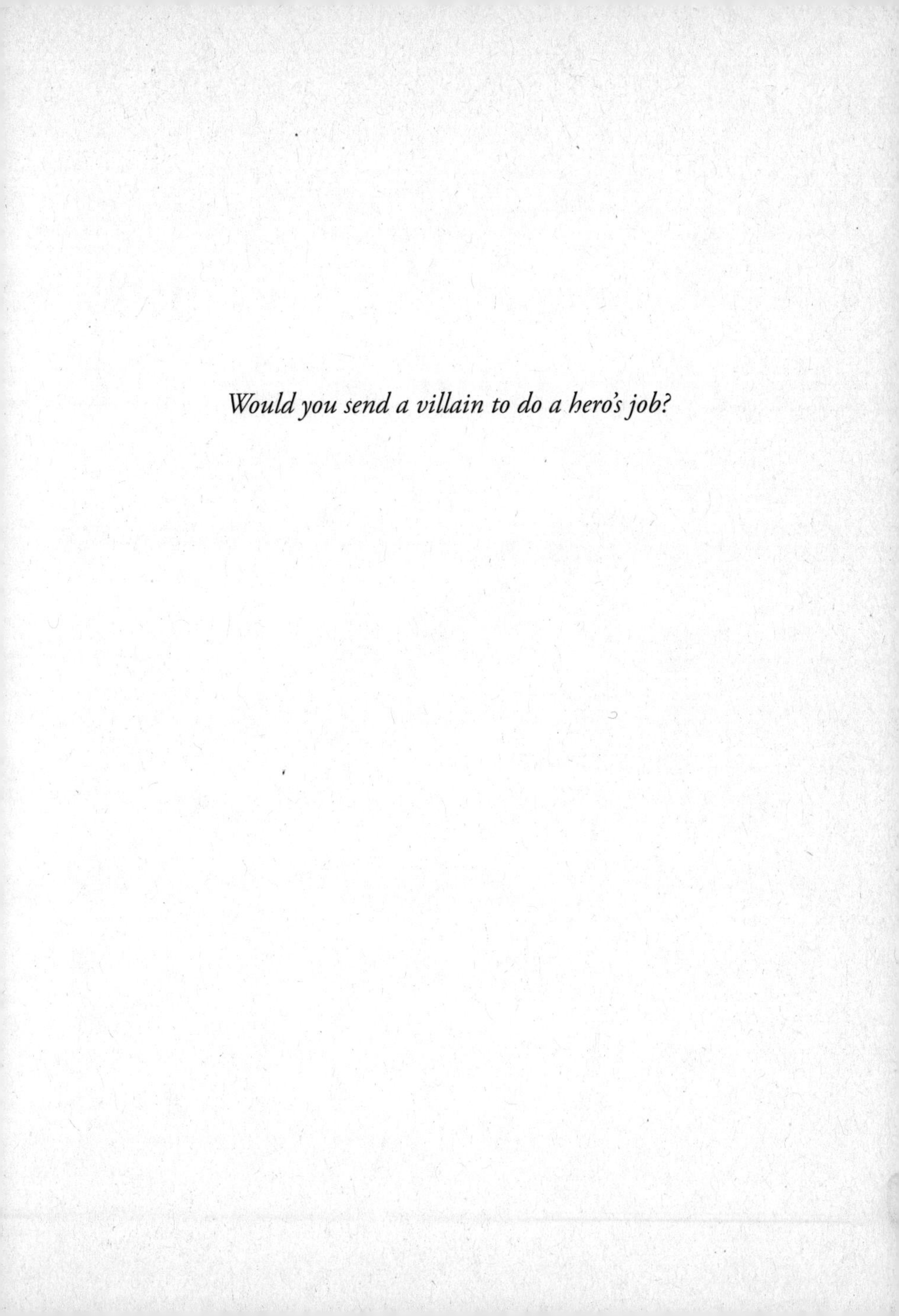

Would you send a villain to do a hero's job?

Happily Ever After Scrolls

Brought to you by FairyWeb—magically appearing on scrolls throughout Enchantasia for the past ten years!

Fairy Tale Reform School Celebrates Its Fifth Anniversary!

by Beatrice Beez

Poison apples, the sleeping curse, becoming a wolf's supper—five years ago, the citizens of Enchantasia quaked in fear at such evildoing. Well, no more! Thanks to one formerly despised villain, wickedness and criminal behavior are being wiped off the map.

"In the days following Cinderella's wedding, no one would even sell me a loaf of bread," says Flora, the princess's stepmother. Yes, that Flora. The one and only stepmonster who used Cinderella as unpaid help and tried to trick the prince into marrying one of her other daughters.

After Cinderella's misfortune became public, Flora was mortified. "I did some wicked things after Cinderella's—pardon me, *Princess Ella's*—father died," says Flora. "I was a terrible example for my two daughters. If we wanted to show our faces in Enchantasia again, I knew we had to change—especially me. From that revelation, FTRS was born."

Fairy Tale Reform School is the education program for the wicked and criminally mischievous that Flora created. It has won praise from Princess Ella herself for its success in turning villains into productive members of society. "Flora's transformation is astonishing," Princess Ella told *Happily Ever After Scrolls* exclusively. "I look forward to seeing their good works continue."

The school's roster of former students turned teachers is huge! There's the Wolf (the esteemed Professor Xavier Wolfington teaches history), the Sea Witch (Madame Cleo is FTRS's etiquette expert), and the Evil Queen (Professor Harlow teaches psychology and runs group therapy sessions).

"Thanks to our teachings, crime in Enchantasia has dropped to an all-time low," Flora says proudly. Since it opened, FTRS has welcomed more than five hundred gnomes, trolls, dwarfs, elves, mer-folk, and other fairy-tale students into its dormitories for grades six through twelve at its campus on the outskirts of Enchantasia near the Hollow Woods.

To celebrate FTRS's fifth anniversary, profiles of FTRS's teachers will be magically popping up on Happily Ever After Scrolls *in the coming weeks. Check your scrolls often for more coverage!*

CHAPTER 1

Picky

Sometimes spying on low-level royals can be so boring.

They're easy to spot the minute they leave their precious royal world behind. With their pricy clothes, made-up faces, and clouds of perfume wafting behind them, girls like that stick out like sore thumbs when they get dropped off in town in their flashy carriages.

So far this afternoon, I've tailed this bunch from the Gnome-olia Bakery (where they made fun of the gnome serving them their rhubarb cupcakes) to the One Enchanted Evening dress shop (where they scoffed at having dresses spun out of cotton even though there is a silk shortage). Neither shop was a good place for me to steal some loot from them.

But at Combing the Sea, which is overflowing with the

most exotic trinkets money can buy, a person could easily be distracted by glittery things…and accidentally "lose" something. There are racks upon racks of fancy hats and veils, and tables piled high with velvet and silk purses and scarves—everything a princess-in-training might need if she doesn't have a fairy godmother to whip it up for her.

But the jewelry and tiaras are what these royals are desperate to get their hands on.

And they haven't even noticed me following them at all. *Ha!*

On the other hand, Neil, the shop owner, has. Trolls are good at sniffing out trouble, and he knows my reputation.

"Need help with something, Gilly?" he asks, eyeing me warily as he polishes the jewelry counter for the fourth time.

"Just looking." I make eye contact so he knows I'm not scared of him. What can he do? So far, I'm just a twelve-year-old potential customer. I can't get kicked out for browsing, can I?

To blend in, I grab a ruby tiara and plop it on my head. I giggle when I see myself in the mirror. Me, the shoemaker's oldest daughter, the tomboy with the frizzy brown hair and freckles, in a tiara! One of the royals turns around and frowns.

Uh-oh. One look at my overalls and she'll know I can't even afford to buy hair ribbons in this place. I've learned that when I'm stealing goods, it's best if my mark barely notices I'm here. I put the mark at ease so she isn't suspicious, then disappear like fairy dust so she can't even remember the color of my hair. Later, when she's filling out a Dwarf Police Squad report, she won't recall anything out of the ordinary about her day.

I smile, which catches the blond off guard. "Where did you find that amazing boa?" I pretend to look through silk throws on the table in front of me. "I've been looking for one just like it. Not that it would look that good on me. It looks gorgeous on you."

Gag.

"Doesn't it?" Blondie grins and turns back to the full-length mirror. "It was the last one though, and I'm definitely taking it. Sorry." She smiles thinly. Blondie doesn't look sorry. I won't be either when her hair clip is mine.

"Oh well." I sigh. "I'll have to find something else to get. Thanks!"

"Good luck." The mini royal wraps the boa around her neck twice. It looks like a giant snake ready to squeeze her. "Pink must be my color," she says as the other girls crowd around her.

"It is!" The others fluff her hair and play with the boa like they are professional royal stylists getting her ready for a ball that evening.

"Try it with your hair up," I suggest, and the other girls nod.

Blondie removes the clip from her hair.

Yes.

I watch what Blondie does next like it's happening in slow motion. This is the moment I've been waiting for. The mini royal drops the glittery golden clip on a table with half a dozen pairs of earrings and forgets all about it.

At least I'm *hoping* she forgets all about it.

That clip is the reason I'm here. I've been following Blondie and her gaggle of friends around all afternoon, waiting for a time to lift it. It has to be worth ten gold coins, at least. Maybe more. Dragon's tooth products are rare in the kingdom of Enchantasia, and smuggling in goods from other kingdoms has gotten harder now that Princess Ella has cracked down on crooks. Yeah, that Princess Ella, otherwise known as Cinderella. She and the other princesses—Snow White, Rose (a.k.a. the expert sleeper), and Rapunzel—all reign over our kingdom together like one big, happy family.

Yeah, right.

I hear the princesses have their own issues co-ruling, but their issues can't compare to those of us in the village—the trolls, ogres, gnomes, fairies, and other creatures that are lumped into the commoner category. Money is tough to come by. I could buy a lot with that one clip Blondie has carelessly tossed aside.

I stare at the clip wistfully, then notice Neil out of the corner of my eye. He's looking at me again. I know better than to make my move yet. I walk to another table and pretend to be interested in magic wand holders. Like I would ever carry a sparkly, pink wand holder. *Eww.*

I notice Blondie pulling up her hair with a ribbon and the girls clapping.

"Much better!" one says and gives her own curls a flip with her hand.

I've always wondered how girls like that get anything done with hair so high-maintenance. Do they spend all day combing their locks? Have to sleep with rollers in their hair? The advertisements for Rapunzel's new hair-care line say her shampoo helps you do away with all that primping. That's why my ten-year-old sister, Anna, wants Rapunzel's shampoo. But I say, what for? At Enchantasia Trade, where I go to school, doing your hair would be a total waste. When you go to shoemaker classes like we do, there is not much need for luminous hair.

Blondie spins around and squeals. "I'm going to get the boa to wear to Petra's thirteenth birthday party."

A snort escapes my lips. *Thirteenth birthday party*. I won't be having one of those. I'll be lucky if Mother has time to make me a cake with all the hours she puts in with Father at the shoe shop. *Uh-oh.* All the girls turn and look at me. So does Neil. I start to cough. "Sorry. I think one of the feathers from your boa flew into my mouth."

Blondie turns to Neil and frowns. "Your boas shed?" She quickly unwraps the one around her neck. "Umm, I think I'll pass then."

"I can assure you," Neil says, his stare at me darkening. "My boas do *not* shed."

That was foolish of me. If Blondie walks out of this shop with her clip, I'll have a tougher time snagging it. People drop things in a place like Combing the Sea all the time. Buying daisies at Everything's Rosy? Not so much. I need to fix this. Time for a distraction.

"Actually, I don't think it was a feather I swallowed," I

say, squeezing into the conversation. "These boas definitely do not shed. My cousin has had a feather skirt from here for years, and it still looks like she just bought it."

"Feather skirt?" Blondie's eyes light up. "Oh, I have to have one of those. Neil, do something with *this*." She drops the boa on the floor and runs to the other end of the store. That's so like a royal.

"I call it first to wear to Laurence's!" says a tall girl with a big nose.

"No fair!" The group heads to the tiny apparel department in the back corner of the shop, and Neil's eyes glow like the gold coins he'll soon be getting. Skirts are way more expensive than boas. See? Neil's lucky to have me. I'm making him money!

I inch my way back toward the table and pick up a crystal hairpin lying next to my clip. I turn it over a couple of times and gaze at it like I'm considering buying it. The girls are still talking about that silly birthday party. I wonder what it would be like to have nothing to worry about other than what filling to pick for my birthday cake.

My hand dangles over the clip.

"Are these made with ostrich feathers?" the tall girl asks Neil.

Closer, closer…

"Ostrich feathers are totally in right now!" Blondie chimes in.

I cover the clip with my hand. It's warm beneath my fingers.

Almost there…

I slide it into the sleeve of my brown jacket with one quick motion.

Success!

I head to the door, making sure to reach up and hold the bell on top so it doesn't jingle when I exit. Then I'm out and heading down the alley next to the shop before anyone even notices I'm gone.

Told you it was easy. Like taking lunch from a sleeping ogre.

CHAPTER 2

The Great Escape

After a mega score like that dragon's tooth comb, I always head home.

No gloating to fellow thieves about my take. No stopping for bread at Gnome-olia Bakery (even if it smells heavenly). And this is definitely not the time to go to the Arabian Nights Pawn Shop to cash in. That is a classic rookie mistake.

Now is the time to blend in, stay out of sight. Disappear.

Never, *ever* run.

Running is like asking to be followed by the dwarf squad and their henchmen. That's Enchantasia's police. Snow White's dwarves got sick of the mines but love their pick-axes, so Snow found them a job where they could still use weapons—law enforcement.

The squad was a joke at first—not many people are afraid of dwarves—but then Princess Ella got wise and hired a bunch of guys who are rumored to be half ogre to be the squad's muscle. Those guys are scary. They could break you in half with their pudgy pinkie fingers. Now crime has gone way down…but it hasn't disappeared. To stay ahead of the ogres, I've had to be smarter about my marks. Royals are still easy targets, but I can't be sloppy.

My eyes scan the village laid out in front of me like a map. I watch as shopkeepers call out end-of-the-day deals (half-price bread, a free shoe shining with any repair, a sale on scarves for the coming winter). I ignore them all, even if my family could use the scarves. Our boot is always cold. I hurry down the cobblestone streets, switching my route home from the way I came this morning. You never want to be seen in the same spot twice when you're in the middle of a caper.

I hurry past the pricier shops and restaurants I wouldn't dare enter because I'm not of royal blood. I pull up the collar of my coat when I walk past the marketplace where commoners are buying their nightly fish or fresh vegetables from farmers. I skip the row where magical goods are being illegally traded. The dwarf squad is undercover in that row all the time.

When I enter the busy town square, I exhale slightly. With so many people and carriages around, it's easy to blend in. Schoolchildren from the Royal Academy are carelessly throwing their coins in the fountain. (Thief tip: Never steal from those waters. They're always being watched.) Someone from *Happily Ever After Scrolls* is trying to sell mini magical scrolls (their latest invention) and is drawing a crowd. A carriage driver is offering rides home for two pence, and royal carriages are lined up in the valet area waiting to take the royals' loot home. One look at the dimming skyline and you remember where your place is in Enchantasia. We commoners live down in the village, while high on the hill, the silver turrets of Royal Manor gleam bright as if to say, "You'll never climb your way up here."

I hear a neigh and then a "whoa," and I turn back toward the fountain, quickly pulling my hood over my head.

"You there!" I freeze. "Have you seen anyone running through the square with a green satchel?" says Pete, the chief of the dwarf squad, in a deep voice that makes him sound much more menacing than he looks. "The baker has lost his shipment for Royal Manor, which was waiting on his steps to be taken to the castle."

I picture Pete high on his horse, looking tough although he isn't even three feet tall on the ground. With his pudgy midsection (he likes cinnamon rolls) and long black beard, he resembles a troll. But his wide, red nose and oversized ears remind me he's a dwarf. The two of us have a love-hate relationship. I've gotten out of a few jams by feeding him info about other thieves, but when I catch a big haul, he comes after me hard.

"Nah," says the small boy standing right next to me. "Haven't seen nuthin'."

Pete sighs, and I exhale. "You mean 'I haven't seen *anything.*' Schools these days," he mumbles. "Okay, go about your business. Find Olaf if you hear of anything." I hear Pete kick the horse's sides with his small feet, and he gallops off into the square.

I reach into the pocket of my overalls Mother just patched and give the boy two pence. "Thanks, kid," I say, patting the satchel under my cloak. I lifted that this afternoon when the royals left the bakery. No surprise it took Pete 'til now to realize it was gone.

Then I disappear through a narrow alleyway off the square that leads to the smaller, poorer streets on my side of town where oversized teacups, boots, and thatched huts replace the nicer brick buildings. The streets are already dark—we don't have lanterns to light the way—but I would know this trail blindfolded. I hurry past the panhandler, dropping a biscuit into his outstretched hand, and move toward the smell of shoe polish that always leads me home. My boot is one of four on this tiny block. With one last look around to make sure I am not being followed, I turn the key and head inside.

"*Gilly!*" My four-year-old twin brothers, Han and Hamish, knock me backward into the door I just came through. They're so light, they roll off me. I see they got into the shoe polish again. There is black all over their cheeks, foreheads, and identical plaid rompers.

"What did you get?" Six-year-old Trixie, with her rosy cheeks and bright red hair, runs into the room at the sound of the collision. "Jam? Cheese? That good pepperoni you got last week?"

"Shh..." Felix, my five-year-old brother, hushes her as he comes down the ladder from the loft where we all sleep in bunk beds. Felix is the wise-beyond-his-years one and looks the most like Father. His dark brown eyes seem to see right through me. "You didn't get caught, did you?"

"No," I assure him and lift my cloak to reveal a satchel full of dinner rolls. My siblings try to grab some. "Wait!" I say, looking around the room. We can barely fit in the living room despite only having a fireplace and one shabby couch.

The walls of the boot have patches to keep out the cold from cracks in the leather exterior. The patches look like paintings, of which we have none. A single drawing of a field of lilies hangs above our fireplace. My sister Anna drew it one night when we were too cold to sleep. The cuckoo clock on the wall chimes six, and I know Father will be home from the shop soon. "Where's Mother?"

"Mother is in the kitchen with Anna, finishing her birthday cake," Trixie says. "Do you want me to go around the back of the boot, knock, and leave the rolls there again?"

"Yes, after you've each eaten a roll first." I open the satchel again and let them each take a roll. They devour the bread within seconds.

The shoe business isn't what it used to be, and money is scarce. Sure, we have three meals, if you call half a cup of chicken broth a meal. If it weren't for my hauls from the market, my siblings would waste away. Instead, the twins finally have a little weight on them, and the dark rings around Trixie's eyes have disappeared.

I do what I can to help out around here. And that includes making sure my siblings are fed enough and get a birthday gift. I could buy a lot with that dragon tooth clip I stole today, but the minute I saw it, I knew I was going to keep it for Anna. The green in the clip matches her eyes, and I could picture her using it to pull back her long hair. She will never let that clip out of her sight, unlike that spoiled royal. That's for sure.

That's why I targeted Blondie today. I only pluck from people who can afford to lose things. Royals can *definitely* afford to lose a few trinkets. So can the baker whose business is booming and who treats Mother poorly whenever she comes in to see if he has any day-old bread on sale. The royals are part of the reason we live in this overcrowded boot, so I don't feel bad taking from them.

"Gilly? Is that you?" I hear Mother's voice and quickly give Trixie the satchel to deposit on the back steps.

Mother looks tired as she comes over to give me a hug, smelling like a mixture of flour and leather, which means she must have had to help Father in the shop earlier. I sink into her like I would a soft pillow.

"You okay?" she asks. Her blue eyes look tired. "Your cheeks are flushed."

"Fine," I say. "I just hurried home from studying so I wouldn't miss the cake."

"How do you think you did on your test?" Mother asks.

How hard can a test on shoe polishes be? I took it and then left school for the rest of the day to find Anna's present. "Great," I say with enthusiasm. "Probably got an A."

"You're home." Anna removes her apron. She has flour on her cheeks and in her brown curls. She's wearing that Rapunzel perfume I snagged her a few weeks back—and claimed it was a free sample. (Anna hates my thieving.) "You're just in time for cake!"

"Cake? What happened to presents first?" I tease.

Mother looks downward. "Gillian, you know business has been slow."

"That doesn't mean magic hasn't found its way to our boot!" I try to sugarcoat everything for my brothers and sisters. "Look what I found near the Pegasus stables this afternoon." I pull the comb out of my pocket, and they gasp. "It practically begged to be rescued." Anna reaches out to touch the golden comb as if she can't believe it's real. "I guess it was meant for you."

"Someone dropped it," Anna says, being her noble self. "We should find the owner."

"Nonsense!" I put the comb in her open palm. "Finders keepers, losers weepers. Isn't that what Hamish says?" Anna doesn't look convinced. "I asked one of the stable guys if he knew whose it was," I improvise. "He didn't and said I should keep it."

Anna's face lights up. "Really?" Mother smiles as Anna uses the comb to pull her curls to one side. She runs to the small mirror near the door. "It's so pretty! Thank you, Gilly!"

I'm about to say "You're welcome" when I hear the lock turn. Father is home. My siblings hurry across the creaky floorboards and stand near the front door. Mother brushes off her apron, and Anna jumps to her place next to her. We all line up like we're a processional at a ball. "Hello, Father," we say as if on autopilot. Mother does too.

"Family," Father says as he hands Mother his hat and cloak to hang up. The smell of shoe polish radiates off him like stinky perfume. "Are we ready to eat?"

"Yes," Mother says. "You can go in first, and I'll feed the children after."

I bite my lip. Father always gets to eat alone and takes the biggest portion. Mother says he needs his strength and quiet after working so hard. I hear Han's stomach growl.

"Okay," Father says, stopping to ruffle my brothers' heads and kiss Trixie and Anna. When he sees me, he freezes. "Gillian."

"Father." I bow my head. The two of us are not on the best of terms these days. He's tired of getting visits from Pete, and I'm tired of us going hungry. Neither of us is willing to budge.

He's barely squeezed his way past us to get to the kitchen when we hear the knock at the door. Anna and I lock eyes, and my stomach drops. My brothers and Trixie look at me. I pretend to fluff pillows on the couch. Dust appears in the air from where I hit a pillow.

"Felix, please get the door." Father squeezes past us all again to greet our visitor.

I try to stay calm. There is no way I was trailed. But the door creaks open and my worst fears are confirmed: Pete and Olaf are here. Pete walks in without being invited. Olaf is so huge he has to duck his bald head under the rafters. I'm not even sure he's going to fit in the room. We all move back so they can squeeze in. I try to appear cool and aloof.

Father reaches for Pete's hand and shakes it. "Good to see you, Peter. Olaf."

"Hi, Hal," Pete says solemnly. Olaf grunts. "Sorry to bother you this late in the evening. Are those work boots I ordered almost finished?"

He's here about a boot order! I relax and almost chuckle. I'm so paranoid.

"Yes, should be done by tomorrow." Father bows. I feel my cheeks flush. Father believes commoners must bow to law enforcement because they work for royals. We are at the bottom of the barrel. Father has always believed a person's class in life is their class. You can't change it. You shouldn't want to change it. All you can do is respect it.

I totally disagree.

"I wish I could say that's the only reason I'm here," Pete says and looks right at me. "Good evening, Gillian. How was your day?"

"Nice, Pete," I say. "Have you gotten taller?"

He grimaces.

Father glares at me. The only sound is our cuckoo clock. "What has she done?"

"Of course you'd take his side," I mutter under my breath. Father may not warm up to me the way he does to a hot cinnamon bun, but I still hate letting him down.

"Have you given me a reason to think otherwise, Gillian?" he asks. Father is a tall man, as tall as Olaf, but unlike Olaf, he looks tired. Working fourteen-hour days in that shoe shop and then coming home to six kids will do that to a person, I suppose. "First it was that pocket watch you took from the King's page, then it was the book from Belle's library—"

"*Borrowed*," I correct him. "Belle said that was a library, so I borrowed a book. I was going to bring it back."

Maybe.

Father rubs his forehead. "I don't know what to do with you anymore." He looks at Pete for backup. "All I do for this child and it's never enough."

"If it were enough, Mother wouldn't have trouble putting dinner on the table every night," I jump in, unable to contain my anger. "Too bad we can't eat shoe leather."

"That's enough!" Father's voice starts to rise.

Pete spots Anna and points to her hair. "Gee, that is

a pretty hair thingamajiggy. Looks expensive. Possibly of dragon origin, wouldn't you say, Olaf?"

"It was a gift," Anna says stiffly. "Gilly found it on the ground."

"*Found* it," Pete repeats. "I guess that's the only way anyone in this boot could afford a piece of jewelry like that." Olaf and Pete chuckle, and it takes all my willpower not to deck them both. My parents say nothing. "Gillian is a lucky girl."

"I didn't steal it, if that's what you're getting at," I snap. "It was just lying on the ground by the Pegasus stables."

"You mean like this satchel?" Pete pulls the green satchel of rolls from behind his back, and Hamish lets out a sob. Our dinner. "We *found* this on your back steps. It looks a lot like the one that went missing this morning at Gnome-olia Bakery. I guess that's a coincidence." Olaf pushes past Trixie to muscle his way to me. "Come clean, Gillian." Pete's beady eyes darken. "You stole that hair clip from a royal at Combing the Sea. Neil, the shop owner, places you there five minutes before the royal realized it was missing."

Fiddlesticks. I'm busted, but my best bet is to stick to my story. "I don't know what to tell you. Maybe the girl has the same clip as the one I found."

"Gilly?" I hear Anna's soft voice and turn to see her disappointed face. "You didn't find this, did you?" I can't lie to Anna. So I don't say anything. "Here." Anna takes the clip from her hair with trembling hands and hands it to Pete. "This doesn't belong to me."

"Sorry, kid." He scratches his beard, which hangs all the way down to his knees, and looks at me greedily. "This is your third offense. You know what that means."

I feel the color drain from my face. "*Second* offense! Those golden eggs came rolling down the hill toward me at the Fairy Festival, I swear."

Pete gives Olaf the handcuffs to put on me. Han and Hamish start to wail.

"I'm taking you in," Pete says. "Headmistress Flora already got your order approved." He hands my parents an eggplant-colored scroll I've seen only twice before. Both times were when thieves got hauled off to FTRS. I've never seen either kid again.

Mother shakily unspools the scroll to read it, and Father takes it from her hands. I look over their shoulders to read it myself.

URGENT MESSAGE

FOR HAL AND EVA, PARENTS OF GILLIAN COBBLER:

Your daughter GILLIAN COBBLER has been taken into custody for the third time for PETTY THEFT. By order of the Enchantasia Dwarf Police Squad, this REPEATED OFFENSE requires that she be taken to Fairy Tale Reform School immediately.

Please pack a bag for Gillian with any personal items she will need for an extended stay.

Headmistress Flora, FTRS
MESSAGE APPROVED BY: Princess Ella

I feel Olaf click the cool metal around my wrists in front of me, and my heart drops.

"Here's the school brochure too." Pete gives one to Mother, who immediately opens it and starts reading. I can see the school's crest on the front of the pamphlet.

"Don't take Gilly!" Han cries, gripping the bottom of my overalls. Hamish throws himself on me along with Trixie. Felix looks sad.

Tears stream down Anna's face. "This has to be a mistake! Tell them it was an accident," Anna begs me. "You didn't mean to take the hair clip, right?" Her eyes are so wide and innocent, which only makes me feel worse. But seeing Pete's smug face makes something inside me snap.

"Maybe I did mean to take that clip," I say defiantly, and Father glares at me. "I had no choice! The shoe shop is doing terribly. We don't have enough money to eat!"

"Gilly!" Mother wrings her hands. "We do not talk about family matters in public."

"We're fine," Father tells Pete and Olaf. "The shoe business isn't what it used to be, but it's fine." Father is furious with me, I can tell.

"You should pack her a bag," Pete tells my mom. "Don't forget her toothbrush. This one is going to be there a while."

Father couldn't care less if I go. My only hope is Mother. "You know me," I plead. "Don't let them take me away. I messed up, but I'm no villain."

Mother's face crumbles. "Not yet, but you could become one if you don't start changing your ways." My jaw drops, and her cheeks burn. "You say you're trying to help us, but you're so focused on the royals and what they have. That hatred worries me." She looks down at her apron. "And besides, the brochure says the school has wonderful classes. They'll be much more interesting than the ones you're in at trade school," she says brightly. "Maybe now you'll really learn something and won't feel the need to skip out."

Pete snorts. "She'll regret the day she skips a class at FTRS. I'll tell you that." Pete gruffly pushes me toward the door, sidestepping the coatrack.

"I'm sorry, guys," I say to my sniveling siblings. I won't look at my parents. I try to sound upbeat. "I'll see you soon, okay?"

Pete snorts. "Doubt that." He grabs the back of my shirt and I elbow him in the ribs. "Ow!"

"*Gilly!*" Father scolds.

"Like I said, you won't be leaving FTRS for a while," Pete seethes. "Which is great news for me, bad for you. You, my little thief, are off to Fairy Tale Reform School."

Chapter 3

Time to Face the Music

"Let me go, Olaf!" I bark as the big guy swings me through the giant oak doors at Fairy Tale Reform School and drops me on the marble floor with a loud thud.

Ouch!

That's the second time he's dropped me today. The first time was when he put me in the carriage to take me to FTRS. If this is how they treat minor criminals, I can't imagine what they'd do if they came across Alva, the fairy who cursed Princess Rose to all those years of slumber.

"Get these handcuffs off me," I yell as Pete stands there calmly, chewing on a piece of taffy. He looks like he's enjoying my tantrum. "I know my rights! I'm only twelve. You're not supposed to handcuff me!"

"Normally we're not supposed to cuff a kid, but you can't be trusted," Pete grumbles. "Last time I let you go, a ruby ring mysteriously disappeared from a visiting queen's fat finger not five minutes later!"

"I have no clue what you're talking about." That pick freaked me out, but it bought us enough food to last a month. No regrets there.

"The handcuffs stay until the boss lady gets here," Pete says.

Headmistress Flora. I've seen Ella's stepmother in the village. That woman never cracks a smile. I might as well enjoy whatever "freedom" I have left. "Can you help me up at least?" I ask Pete. He nods to Olaf, who lifts me by my armpits. I shrug out of his grasp and take a look around the giant hall.

So this is what Fairy Tale Reform School looks like. Having heard the rumors all these years, I was expecting to see kids handcuffed to walls and torture chambers. The woman who runs this place supposedly made her own daughters cut off part of their feet to fit into Ella's precious glass slipper, so I wouldn't put anything past her. But if she's hiding a torture chamber in this building, it's not in the swanky foyer.

I can't let my guard down, but I have to say...

This place looks cushy! The outside is. It took the carriage at least ten minutes to get from the gates to the castle, which is surrounded by a moat. Olaf said the moat is filled with hungry crocs to keep kids from escaping, but I think he was trying to scare me.

I hope.

The castle doesn't look creepy at all—well, if you ignore the fact that there are some gargoyle statues hanging around. With its trio of tall towers, a mint-green roof, and ivy and rainbow-colored flowers everywhere, it rivals the courtyard of Royal Manor. Even the doors Olaf tossed me through were pretty—pale green with strange hand-carved panels that show pictures of a full moon, an apple, a trident, and a glass slipper.

The inside is inviting too. Olaf won't let me go far, but I can make out a large fireplace in the sitting room that looks quite toasty. Velvet couches and leather chairs perfect for reading surround the fire and are also tucked into nooks next to large stained glass windows. Candles are burning everywhere. Some are scented, which make me a bit woozy, and a bit hungry too. I can hear light music playing in the distance—something classical—but this room is silent, empty, and spacious. *Ahhh.* I take a moment to enjoy the space. Then I spot a large, gold sign above the doorway to the sitting room.

I burst out laughing. Are they serious? Turn a villain into a hero? That would be like asking a mermaid to morph into an ogre! I laugh harder, holding my belly, which is growling now that I missed what little we would have had for dinner.

The boot my family lives in gives new meaning to the

word "cozy," but this place is huge! My sisters and brothers could go wild without ever worrying about knocking over a candle and setting our boot on fire. It's sort of fancy though, which could be a problem for Han and Hamish. I've never seen so many golden chandeliers and mirrors in my life. Large mirrors; small, ornately framed, creepy, jeweled ones; and a massive oval one with a purple gilded frame that hangs in the two-story entrance. I sense someone here is a mirror collector.

I lean in to the purple mirror. My frizzy brown hair and oval-shaped eyes that look nothing like Mother or Father's are reflected back at me. Mother says I got Father's stubborn chin, which juts out when I'm making a point. According to her, I'm always trying to make a point. I think I'm doing that right now actually. I look closer. Is that a hair sticking out of my chin? How did that get there? I should pluck it. I look like the old peddler that tried to trick Snow White. I lift my handcuffed hands to my chin and attempt to yank the hair out, but it won't budge. Pete looks at me like I'm crazy. I lean even closer, my nose practically touching the glass.

"Do you mind?" a voice inside the mirror snaps.

I jump back. "Sorry! I didn't realize this mirror was…occupied."

"Show some respect," says Pete, who is leaning against the far wall peeling an apple with a pocketknife. "That's Miri the Magic Mirror you're talking to."

"Miri?" I look closer at the mirror and still only see my reflection. But wow, I've heard of this mirror. Everyone has! Seeing it is like spotting a princess in the flesh. If you cared about that sort of thing, which I don't. "I thought you lived in Royal Manor with Ella and the other princesses."

The mirror snorts. She seems as snobby as the royals. "You think those are the only places I hang? I can come and go between mirrors as I please—unlike you, my little thief, once you're checked in here."

"Who said I'm a thief?" I ask as I use a bobby pin (a crook's best friend) hidden in my shirtsleeve to pick the lock on my handcuffs. I hear a little click and *ahh*...the cuff grips loosen. I keep them on though so Pete doesn't make them tighter.

I walk away from prying Miri the Magic Mirror and find myself in front of a rack of FTRS brochures. I pick up the one titled *Parents' Guide*. I open to the first page and read the top line: "How to Know If Your Child Should Be Enrolled at Fairy Tale Reform School." I read the letter that follows from the school headmistress, glancing hard at the line that reads: "The path between right and wrong can easily be blurred in a fairy-tale community where magic and wishes can be used in ways that can turn good children into wicked ones." The headmistress goes on to list what she calls "warning signs for delinquent behavior." I wonder how I match up.

Constant lying. Check!

Unexplained, frequent absences. Check!

Anger over one's class in life. Well…the royals' privileges do set me off sometimes, so I figure I have another check for that one.

Bullying. No check. I never roughed anyone up in my life.

Turns friends into toads. No check. (How mean would that be?)

Thieving. A fourth check.

I check my score.

"Three or More Checks: Signs your child should be enrolled at FTRS immediately."

Ugh! What does this headmistress know about my life? I had good reasons for my stealing. I cram the brochure back in the stack and walk away, stopping next in front of a wall of photos. There's a picture of students smiling in a potion-making class while something green and fizzy bubbles out of a bottle nearby...another of boys flying on Pegasi through the sky above the school...kids fencing...students in front of a crystal ball...the list goes on.

Next to the school photos is a plaque: FTRS Esteemed Graduates. Underneath are photos of teens out in the real world. Some girl got an internship at the Fairy Fashion Institute of Design. That's pretty cool. A guy in goggles is working part-time at the Enchantasia Elfin Science Institute. Not too shabby. My eyes fall on the third picture. It's of a girl working with Ella's fairy godmother. The photo is of them conjuring up glass slippers. I feel my blood begin to boil.

"Copycat!" I yell at the picture, hoping for a reply.

"What are you talking about?" Miri sounds almost bored.

"This picture!" I say bitterly. "This is the whole reason I'm stuck here in the first place. My family would be more than fine if the princesses hadn't given Ella's fairy godmother all the formal-wear shoe orders. Now whenever someone wants a glass slipper for a proposal or a ball, she just poofs them up!"

"The pink ones are gorgeous!" Miri chimes in. "I ordered a pair just to look at."

"Hey! You will not disgrace one of our princesses by speaking of her like this," Pete tells me. "She is royalty and doesn't have to explain her reason for doing things."

"She owes us!" I complain. "My father came up with the glass slipper, and then her lousy fairy godmother ripped it off and took all the credit."

I think of all we've given up since Ella's shoe policy changed. How much my brothers and sisters have done without. That's why I started stealing. Not to hurt people, but so I could bring in the extra cash Father no longer could. I was trying to help. But my parents don't see it that way, and I'm not sure they ever will.

"Rapunzel wore my father's shoes to the Once Upon a Time ball two years ago," I tell Pete. "He was so pleased when *Happily Ever After Scrolls* said everyone should have a pair of those pink pumps. Father could have made good money with those shoes, but instead, Ella lets her fairy godmother just copy them with a poof of her wand." I don't care that my voice is echoing in the grand foyer. "It's not fair."

"No, it's not," I hear someone say, her footsteps barely more than a whisper against the floor. "But then again, a lot in life isn't fair." The woman is concealed in the shadows.

"It's how you handle yourself in such situations and what you learn from them that will define you. That's what you'll learn to master during your time here."

An older woman steps out of the shadows and I see a thin smile spread across her lips. It's her. Princess Ella's formerly wicked stepmother in the flesh.

Happily Ever After Scrolls

Brought to you by FairyWeb—magically appearing on scrolls throughout Enchantasia for the past ten years!

From Pond Scum to Headmistress: Flora Leads FTRS

by Beatrice Beez

It isn't easy being the most despised woman in Enchantasia. Just ask Flora. Five years ago, she couldn't leave Galmour Castle without being pelted with rotten radishes.

And that was on a good day.

After Miri the Magic Mirror showed Flora the torture she put Ella through, Flora vowed to change her ways. "I still can't talk about the glass slipper incident without getting upset, but I will say that I did not encourage my girls to cut off part of their feet to fit in a shoe! I'm not insane!" Flora insists.

Self-help books and meditation helped Flora realize that the pain she inflicted on Ella was the same she went through as a child. Flora spent her days taking care of her siblings. She never had time for friends. "Mother only gave her love to my sister Anastasia, who was fair-haired and blue-eyed."

Flora escaped by accepting an arranged marriage proposal and had two daughters. When the marriage failed, she met Rufus, Ella's father. That's when Flora's life felt complete. "Those first few years we were all very happy together," she says.

Then the green monster of jealousy took over. Flora began obsessing about how much Ella looked like Anastasia and worried that Rufus only cared about his own little girl. "I can never take back what I did, but I will spend the rest of my life trying to make it up to Ella," Flora says.

After her transformation, she sought Ella's blessing to tear down Galmour Castle and create Fairy Tale Reform School on that very spot. "I wanted to help others avoid the same destructive path," Flora says. She sought out and mentored some of Enchantasia's most villainous criminals, many of whom are now staff members at the school.

She has even seen a change in her girls. "They are much more compassionate. The three of us can finally look at Miri the Magic Mirror (who advises part-time at the school) and feel good about ourselves," Flora says.

We're sure Princess Ella would approve. Rumors have swirled for months that the princess is going to make a public show of support for her stepmother by throwing an anniversary ball in the school's honor. Check your Happily Ever After Scrolls for more ball updates!

CHAPTER 4

Home Sweet Home?

So this is what the stepmonster looks like.

I've never met Headmistress Flora before. Her long, thin face and pointy nose; dark, tiny eyes; and sweeping black-and-white hair don't exactly soften her reputation. Still, I'm kind of disappointed there are no lightning bolts shooting out of her hands or devil's horns poking out of her head. The way my buddy Cedric talked about the time his brother got hauled in here, I was sure that's what I would find.

He also said her office looked like a dungeon, which it does not. It looks like a princess threw up in here. The furniture is gold with purple velvet cushions, and there are oriental rugs and crystal vases everywhere. It's kind of how I imagine Ella decorates her castle.

Headmistress Flora interlocks her long fingers under her chin and stares at me with interest over her mahogany desk. "I have been waiting for the pleasure of this meeting for a long time."

I smile. "Really? I can't say the same."

Headmistress Flora, however, is not fazed. "I'm sorry to hear that, but nonetheless, I've been expecting you. The police commissioner has kept me abreast of your, shall we say, extracurricular activities."

I try not to laugh. Extracurricular activities—why have I never thought of calling it that?

"I knew it was only a matter of time before you made your way to our doors," Flora tells me. "I think we can do wonders for you. Our etiquette classes, history lessons, and behavior training are geared toward children who have problems just like you."

My eyes narrow. "What do you mean *problems*?"

"Your issues with authority," the headmistress says. "You have no respect for your elders. My own girls were the same way." She turns a frame toward me, and I see Ella's stepsisters, Azalea and Dahlia. The girls are dressed in gowns as gorgeous as Snow White's. Their makeup is flawless, and their hair is done with Rapunzel's finest hair extensions. If I didn't know better, I would think they were royals.

"It took a lot of reflection and meditation—which we offer here—but eventually my girls saw the error of their selfish ways. Now they attend the Royal Academy. They are some of the only commoners to do so," she brags. "Wouldn't you like your problems to vanish like theirs did?"

My frown deepens. "Look, lady. I'm hungry. I want to feed and protect my family. If FTRS could help me do that, I would have snuck in a long time ago."

Kids don't really buy this garbage, do they? I mean, how can a *school* change me into a whole new person? Will I ever not want my siblings to have the things they deserve? Or not wish Mother had an easier life and a bigger shoe to live in? I doubt it.

"Is that why you take things? To make money?" the headmistress asks me.

I play with the fraying hem of my overalls. "Who doesn't want more money?" I challenge her. "I do it to buy things we need, okay? And I only take things from royals who won't even notice anything's missing."

"Whether or not people miss things is not the point,"

Flora tells me. “You’re taking something that does not belong to you. Today it may be a dragon’s tooth clip, but tomorrow it could be a carriage. Where does it end? Before long, your face is on Wanted posters throughout the land.”

“You mean like Alva and Gottie?” I ask.

I’m talking, of course, about the infamous villains in hiding—Alva, the cranky fairy who cursed Sleeping Beauty (Stay away from those spinning wheels!), and Gottie, Rapunzel’s kidnapper (Here’s a nice tower we can lock you in forever!). Being drop-dead gorgeous and royal seems to come with a lot of baggage.

While I’ve heard there are occasional Gottie sightings, Alva has been missing for years. Rumor is she’s dead, but I doubt Enchantasia is that lucky.

“People need to want to be saved,” Flora tells me. “Sadly, Alva is untraceable, and Gottie has not committed to reform. But we *will* bring them in.”

Maybe she thinks I need her to say that so I’ll sleep better, but I sleep just fine, thank you.

“Is that what you want for your own life?” Flora asks. “To be an outlaw?”

I snort. “Your scare tactics don’t worry me. You can’t keep me here forever.”

"Oh, I'm afraid I can, my dear." Without hesitation, Flora produces a proclamation no one showed me before. The long scroll has Flora's signature, Pete's…and my parents'?

I sit back up. "What's this?"

"Permission to hold you until I see positive changes in your behavior." Flora watches my reaction. "I had the scroll messengered over after your arrest. Keep this attitude up and you could be here indefinitely."

I wonder if Flora gets a kick out of moments like these. "My parents agreed to hold me here *forever*? This place is for real criminals." I stand up I'm so outraged. "I allegedly took a dragon's tooth clip! That's not a big deal!" Flora stares at me sadly.

"Since your thefts were not violent crimes, you will have the freedom to move around school as you please and can choose extracurricular activities like our Pegasus flying lessons." Flora looks at me. "We want to get to the root of why you're thieving."

"How long am I stuck here?" I ask.

"Once we feel you have successfully mastered the right behavior skills and knowledge to be an upstanding resident of Enchantasia, you will be released," Flora says.

Clever. She didn't really answer the question. "When can I see my family?"

Flora frowns. "I'm afraid visitation is not allowed. We find the pull of home makes it hard for students to concentrate. They can visit you around the same time as the school anniversary ball we're hoping to host. If you're doing well, they are welcome to attend too."

Who cares about a stupid ball? "No thanks. I just want to get out of here and back to my brothers and sisters."

"Exactly my point," Flora says. "That's why you need FTRS right now. If you don't change, they won't either. Is this the life you want for them someday?"

My stomach feels squishy inside. Threatening the well-being of those rug rats is the ultimate weapon when it comes to me. I would never do anything to hurt them. Just thinking about Felix or Trixie stealing things makes me sicker than eating a tuna sandwich.

"No," I admit. "But I don't need reform school!" My eyes narrow. "Reform school is for stepmonsters who lock kids away and make them clean the toilet!"

I see a flash of anger in Headmistress Flora's eyes, but she doesn't lash out. "Perhaps I should give you a moment to think about what you want to say next." She purses her lips and rises from her cushy chair. "I wouldn't want us to start off on such unpleasant terms."

Flora leaves the room, and I'm all alone. I stare at the shiny desk in front of me and contemplate a life on the run. That gold quill set on Flora's desk could get me enough money to make it at least to Parrington. There is no way I'm staying in this place. I stuff the quill in my overalls pocket. That's when I hear someone laugh.

"Nice score! Wow, you seem pretty spunky for a human. I like that."

I jump up and spin around. "Who said that?" I don't see anyone in the office. "Miri?" I knock on the mirror in Flora's office. Miri said she could jump mirrors. She must be listening in. Maybe she saw me steal that quill. Fiddlesticks.

"God, no!" A girl my own age slips out from behind one of the tall lamps in the corner of the office and half runs, half floats over to me. How did she hide behind something so narrow? "Miri's on break right now, which is why I'm in here." She walks around the desk and I notice two almost transparent wings sticking out of her back. They're fluttering at top speed. "Rule number one about FTRS: Always know

Miri's schedule. That mirror can get you in big trouble." She holds out her hand. "Kayla."

I stare at her hand but don't shake it. I agree with Father on one thing—people aren't nice to you without a reason. "What do you want?"

Kayla doesn't look ruffled, even though her wings stop moving for a second. "Nothing."

"So why are you spying on me?" I ask.

She smiles coyly. "I'm not spying. I came to swipe a scroll so I could get a message to someone, but I heard Pete bring you in and had to see what the fuss was about. Usually no one fights once they get thrown in these doors, but you..." She folds her arms across her chest and takes me in from all angles. "I'm impressed. I can't believe you've avoided the joint this long after getting caught stealing three times! You must be some kind of genius."

"You go here?" I ask, mystified by this pixie of a girl in front of me. She's my height, but so petite that she looks like she could break in half. Her short blond hair only makes her look smaller, as does the pale blue jumper she's wearing. It must be a school uniform because the crest on the chest has the letters *FTRS*. "What are you in for?"

Kayla waves her hand. "I was caught using fairy magic for personal gain, and my family got all bent out of shape about it." She rolls her eyes. "Is there anything wrong with wanting the baker's son to have a crush on you? I think not!"

"You're a fairy?" I can't help but be skeptical. "I thought fairies were tiny."

Kayla fiddles with one of her oversized amber earrings, which match her eyes. "We can be tiny when we need to be, but I'm not supposed to fly 'til I'm twenty-one, so I usually stay normal size." She rolls her eyes. "My mother is a stickler about the flying early thing, which is why she was peeved when she caught me flying over Royal Manor. I was already grounded for casting a spell on my sister that made her nose as big as her face. My aunt was able to fix it…eventually." Kayla looks at a portrait on the wall and sighs. "After that, Mother said I was a hazard to everyone around me so she had me committed at FTRS. I've been here for a while now with no parole in sight. That's why I keep flying. Why stop?"

"I thought you could leave whenever your transformation was complete," I say.

Kayla purses her lips. "That's what they tell people, but…"

I try not to let her answer ruffle me. "So how is it?"

The dungeons rumor. Tell me there are no dungeons. Or whips.

"Honestly? It's not bad as schools go. The dungeon is never used," Kayla tells me. Maybe she has ESP. "And we are not chained to the walls or forced to take strange potions to transform us. We do have to wear these itchy uniforms." She points to her own blue jumper. "Basically, FTRS is a boarding school for delinquents. We take etiquette with the Sea Witch. Try taking dancing lessons from a teacher floating in a fish tank.

"The chef makes a mean apple cobbler—without poison apples! The dorms are sweet—they're in the castle turrets and there are only two students to every room. And we have plenty of time to try out activities—fencing, Pegasus flying lessons, snake charming. They like us to tap into new parts of our personalities here."

Apple cobbler, huge rooms, time to try activities? We have none of that at trade school. We have to bring lunch. My sandwich is soggy by the time noon rolls around since Mother makes our lunches at five in the morning. Plus, we get our own bedroom with only one roommate! "This place doesn't sound half bad," I admit.

"It's not," Kayla agrees. "It's fun as long as you stay on

Flora's good side. Make it hard on her, and she'll make things doubly hard on you. She doesn't like it when students step out of line, especially during the first few months. Quit bringing up Ella. Real sore spot. And don't question her about the villains on the lam. Wolfington has been tracking Alva for years and still hasn't sniffed her out."

"Who?" I ask.

"Professor Wolfington," Kayla says as if I should know this. "The Wolf? The one who ate Red's granny? He's everyone's favorite professor—strict, but he actually listens. He's a good guy. Er, I mean wolf. Wolf man." She waves her hand. "Whatever."

The clock on Flora's desk chimes seven, and Kayla flies back to the standing lamp in the corner of the room. "Remember what I said—be nice and your move will go smoothly." Her eyes glow. "Who knows? You might even be my new roomie! My last one went missing a while ago," she says, and before I can ask why…*POOF!* She vanishes.

"I thought you were in for using fairy magic," I whisper.

Kayla's laughter floats through the room. "*Let's say I haven't been reformed yet.*"

I hear the doorknob turn and quickly sit back down.

"*Be nice!*" Kayla reminds me.

A wolf turned professor, a sea witch for an etiquette coach, a delinquent fairy who still uses magic, and an apple cobbler that is killer in a good way?

This place isn't what I thought it would be. I think I can survive FTRS until I figure out my next move.

The door opens, and Flora walks in again.

"So, Gillian," she says. "Do you want to try having this conversation again?"

Thinking of Kayla, I turn to the headmistress with a sad smile. "I know you want what's best for me. And I know I can change with FTRS's help."

Maybe I should take up acting. I wonder if they offer a course in that here.

Flora sort of smiles. And I'm almost positive that somewhere near that standing lamp, an invisible Kayla just winked at me.

CHAPTER 5

The Escape Artist

Pete and Olaf are gone. We all walked to the grand foyer to see them out. ("It's only proper to see a guest off," Flora told me. Some guests they were. They had me arrested!) Then the heavy wooden doors of the front entrance closed behind them. I wasn't sad to see those two go, but now...I'm all alone with the stepmonster. (And possibly Kayla.)

"Well, we should get you settled," Flora says, sounding very un-stepmonster-like. She hands me a heavy stack of papers. The Fairy Tale Reform School insignia is embossed on the top one. "A few rules plus our guidelines for classes and after-school activities," she says. "And of course, our disciplinary actions policy, which I'm sure you won't be needing. But first-, second-, and third-offense consequences are listed here."

I flip through the book quickly. Wow. There are *a lot* of rules. More than Kayla let on. My eyes begin to glaze over. Then I focus on two words I don't like: group therapy.

"What's this?" I ask, pointing to the offensive phrase.

"We find the best way to rehabilitate our students' behaviors is through sessions with a therapist," Flora says. "Professor Harlow handles those, and they are quite rewarding."

"Annoying" would be the word I would choose. Somehow I don't picture the Evil Queen passing out tissues and wanting to talk about our feelings. "And if I refuse to go?" I jut out my chin defensively.

Flora's smile is sort of creepy. "Your stay here will be as long as it needs to be." She waves her hand. "We keep a close eye on our students' behavior modifications."

Hmm...I'm not sure I like the sound of this anymore.

"Ready, Headmistress?" The mirror near us begins to glow, and Miri's voice is loud and clear. I suspect she's been listening the whole time.

"Yes, thank you, Miri," Flora says. "Would you like to see your new room, Gillian? I hope you like bunk beds."

"When you have five brothers and sisters who sleep in

the same boot with you, bunk beds are the only way to fit everyone," I say.

Headmistress Flora nods as if she understands, but I doubt it. Before she built FTRS, she lived here in Galmour Castle. Now she lives in a private wing of the school. She says all the teachers have apartments on campus.

"Well, you won't find our quarters as cramped as your shoe, that's for sure," Flora tells me. "But we do have to find you a roommate. Miri, who do we have available in the girls' dormitory?"

"We have limited choices," Miri says grimly. "There's Sasha, the sprite who keeps chopping off her roommate's hair while she sleeps."

I cringe. I may not love my hair, but I do like the length. "I'm not due for a haircut for a while," I tell Flora.

"Who else do we have?" Flora taps her foot impatiently.

"How about Tara? Her roommate will be in the infirmary all semester because that illegal spell she cast went awry."

"Any other options?" I ask. "I do not make a good guinea pig."

Flora runs a hand through her salt-and-pepper hair and exhales. "Miri, who do we have left?"

I pat the quill in my pocket—I need someone who won't

judge my thieving. "I don't mean to pry, Headmistress, but I saw a paper on your desk about a girl named Kayla needing a new roommate. What about her?"

"Oh God, not that one," Miri mutters.

"Her picture was on the file, and she didn't look like someone who would turn me into a toad."

Flora fiddles with the large brooch on her tailored dress and stares at me doubtfully. "You should know that her last roommate went missing under mysterious conditions. We've found no trace of her."

"Allegedly went missing." Kayla appears from behind a clock. "She was half wolf and had a nasty temper. I'm sure she'll turn up eventually." Kayla looks at me. "Who's this?"

"Gillian Cobbler, our newest student," Flora introduces me. Kayla and I shake hands. Again. "She's in need of a roommate, and for some strange reason, she's requested you." Flora turns to Miri. "We have almost a hundred students and there's no one else? Kayla is still on probation for making it snow in the library last month."

"It looked so pretty," Kayla says with a sigh.

Flora does not look amused. "You were using magic, which you know is forbidden unless it's part of a class assignment."

"Right!" Kayla's eyes soften. "I'm really sorry about that. Won't happen again." She pauses. "So *now* can I have Gilly as a roommate?"

Flora makes a noise resembling a growl.

"Headmistress?" Miri interrupts. "I'm getting called to the castle by Rose."

Oh wow! Rose is Sleeping Beauty. Not that I care about that sort of thing.

"When you're through, please meet me in my office," Flora tells her.

"Yes, Headmistress," Miri says. "Be good, girls." With that, she's gone.

Flora doesn't linger either. "Well, if you're sure..." I nod. "Okay, Kayla can show you to the dormitory and give you a tour on the way."

"Yes, Headmistress," Kayla says. We wait for Flora to walk away. "That was brilliant! I was trying to think of a way to make us roomies."

The hair on my arms stands up. "*Shh!* What if Miri hears you?"

"Please!" Kayla's wings stop fluttering. "If Miri got called to the castle, she is at the castle." Kayla links her arm through mine, and I start to rise. "We have time before dinner to get you unpacked. Let me show you the school first."

"Let's walk," I insist. "I've never flown before. I'm sure it will make me dizzy."

Kayla looks disappointed. "Fine."

Drip. Click. Snap.

"What was that?" The grand foyer is completely empty except for us.

Kayla shrugs. "Beats me. Could be a Pegasus. They're not supposed to fly by the castle. One nicked a turret last week. Everyone else is at after-school activities."

Drip. Click. Snap.

Kayla flies toward the large front doors, and I quickly follow. When we reach the doors, she looks up. In one fast movement, she pulls off her belt and flicks it in the air at the chandelier. The fancy light fixture sways.

"*Aaah!* Kayla, cut it out!"

I jump. There's a boy up there, standing on the crystal chandelier! He has slightly curly blond hair and is wearing a uniform—a navy sweater vest over a white shirt with khaki pants—but his boots are muddy. He's stepping on priceless crystals with cruddy boots? Is he insane?

"Jax! What are you doing up there?" Kayla whispers heatedly.

"I'm cleaning the crystal for Flora," Jax says and rolls his eyes. "What does it look like I'm doing? I'm making a break for it."

Kayla applauds. "Yay! This time I know you can do it."

I shade my eyes from the light bursting through the stained glass window next to the chandelier Jax is perched on. "Busting out? Why?" I ask Kayla. "I thought you said this place was cool."

Jax laughs loudly and looks at me. I feel slightly stunned. I've never seen violet eyes before. "FTRS was fun for a while, but strange things have started happening, and I don't want to be here when something bad goes down."

Strange things? What kind of strange things? Why does Kayla suddenly look pale?

"He's exaggerating," Kayla tells me, but she doesn't sound convincing.

Drip. Whatever Jax is holding is leaking. Kayla and I move out of the way so we don't get wet. "Grease," Jax explains to me. "It lubricates the window." He swings the chandelier, and as it nears the window, he uses a fork to try to pry the window open. "A few more tries and I'll have it."

"Then what are you going to do, genius?" I ask. "You're two stories up."

Jax's eyes gleam. "I've jumped from higher spots before."

"It's true," Kayla says to me. "Jax once jumped from the gym to the dining-hall turret. That was three stories up. We call him the Escape Artist. One time he even managed to break into Azalea's and Dahlia's rooms and borrowed their keys to the indoor pool so the whole dorm could take a midnight swim."

"Impressive," I tell him. "And I thought I was good at tricking obnoxious royals."

"She stole a dragon's tooth clip from one this morning," Kayla fills him in.

"Nice," Jax says. "Your first pull?"

"No, I've been doing it for a while," I brag.

"Me too," Jax says. "My father is a farmer. You can only get so far trading vegetables. I needed to kick things up a notch."

For some reason, I don't think any of us are going to make the transformation Headmistress Flora is looking for. "Why do you want to break out so bad?"

"I've got places to see, and Enchantasia isn't one of them." Jax swings the chandelier so hard the crystals clang together. The window latch pops open, and I watch Jax leap from the chandelier to the tiny window ledge. I'm in awe. Jax looks down at us smugly before pushing open the window. "Are you sure you two don't want to join me?"

"There's no time for us," Kayla says. "Get out of here. Wait!" Her eyes widen. "You deactivated the alarm on the window, right?"

"There isn't one," Jax insists. "If there was, I wouldn't be able to do this." But when Jax lifts the window, we hear:

EEEEEE! EEEE! EEEE! Unauthorized exit! Unauthorized exit!

The shrieking sound is so intense that Kayla and I cover our ears. Within seconds, Flora is out of her office and running toward us.

Swoosh!

I feel something brush past me and whirl around. When I look up at Jax again, a large, muscular man with a long mane of hair is hanging on to the window ledge, his furry hands pulling Jax back by his shirt. How did the man get up there without a ladder?

"Mr. Jax," the man says in a low growl, "we really must stop meeting like this." He pulls Jax from the window ledge, and the two drop to the ground with barely a grunt. This must be the Wolf, and clearly he can jump. "Anything you want to say for yourself? Like what you were doing up there?"

"I needed fresh air," Jax mumbles.

"Ah, same as the last two times." The Wolf's voice is as smooth as butter and very calm, considering what is going on.

I turn to Kayla to suggest we get out of there, but she's gone! Oh man, are you guilty by association in this place? Great. Just great.

"You know what a third offense means, don't you?" Flora says to Jax, who looks like he might throw up. "Solitary confinement for a month."

A month? Geez, that's harsh!

"Please," Jax begs. "Just give me one more chance. I won't try this again…"

"Where were you going?" Flora asks. Jax doesn't answer. "Then you leave me no choice."

"Wait!" I jump in, and they all look at me. The Wolf's eyes are an icy blue that are both terrifying and mesmerizing. We thieves have to stick together. "It's my fault. On the way in earlier, I dropped my journal. I write in it every day and planned on sending letters to my sister." They're still listening. That's good. "I was so upset that I lost it, and Jax offered to try to get on the grounds to go look for it for me." I look at Flora. "Since the doors are locked, he had to break out."

"Is that so?" The Wolf looks amused. "Can you confirm this, Mr. Jax?"

Jax's mouth starts to twitch, but thankfully stops. "Every word of it. I was trying to be the gentleman Madame Cleo is always telling me to be."

The Wolf nods. "Quite noble of you." He looks at Flora. "I guess we should give them both another shot, since this is Miss Gillian's first hour here and Mr. Jax was only trying to—what did you call it?—be a gentleman."

Flora's blood vessels look like they might burst on her forehead. "A *small* shot. After this, they are both held accountable for their actions. Understood?"

Jax and I look at each other. Jax speaks for both of us. "We understand completely."

Happily Ever After Scrolls

Brought to you by FairyWeb—magically appearing on scrolls throughout Enchantasia for the past ten years!

Why We Fear Apples: Meet FTRS's Psychologist, Professor Harlow

by Beatrice Beez

Former Occupation: The Evil Queen of Snow White's nightmares—and ours (Can anyone ever look at an apple the same way again?)—ruled the kingdom of Haddleburg with an iron fist.

Current Occupation: "She's such an intelligent woman that she doesn't need to terrorize people to make an impact," Flora said. (Harlow declined to be interviewed.) Today, Harlow is one of FTRS's strictest professors. She loves pop quizzes, so maybe terrorizing still applies.

Hobbies: Fashion (Jasper's Tailoring is where she orders custom gowns). She also loves to spend time with her sister, Jocelyn, who is an FTRS student, and coach the first-place fencing team.

Strengths: Some say Harlow still dabbles in witchcraft, but Flora says that's nonsense.

Weakness: Her lack of a crown. Sources say that is still a sore spot.

Likes: Beauty. "She's determined to stay young!" says an anonymous student who was worried that Harlow's pet raven, Aldo, would know she was being interviewed. ("He knows everything going on in her world.")

Hates: Being disrespected. "Most of the kids in detention are there because of Professor Harlow," an anonymous student said before hearing a bird squawk and fleeing our interview.

Love life: Need we bring up that poison apple again? Harlow's love affair is solely with her own milky-white reflection. And possibly Aldo.

Check back next week for more FTRS anniversary coverage!

CHAPTER 6

Who's the Real Poison Apple Here?

"Roomie! Jax! Wait up!" Kayla surprises me the next morning when she emerges from a hall that just popped up to the left of us.

As a thief, I'm impressed with the layout of this joint—rooms and walls seemingly shift in front of you almost hourly, making it impossible to come up with a clear escape route. It's like they don't want us to ever be *too* comfortable. I can see I need to stay on my toes and keep my head down if I want to get out of FTRS quickly. I just witnessed two sprites getting hauled off to detention for having a wand battle that lit a chair on fire.

"Are you guys okay?" Kayla whispers hurriedly. She's practically floating, her toes barely touching the ground.

"Did you get detention with the Sea Witch? Don't hate me! I'm sorry I bailed." Her face scrunches up like my brother Hamish's does when he's feeling guilty. "I cannot get my third detention in a month."

"And I can?" Jax asks, slinging his book bag over his shoulder. "If it weren't for your new roomie here, I'd be doing the waltz this afternoon with Madame Crazy. Thankfully, this one can spin a good yarn." Jax high-fives me, and I blush. No one usually compliments me on my lying skills, even if they are stellar.

"She's the best," Kayla seconds and squeezes my arm. Her hand is ice cold.

If I were that great, you'd think Kayla would have slept in our room last night. Instead, I had to find my way to the girls' dorm tower on my own after Professor Wolfington let us go with a warning. Then after I got to the tower, I found a note on the magic chalkboard on our door that said: "Sorry, pulling all-night study session. Have a great first sleep in our room!—K."

"If you're that good at covering for people, maybe you can bail me out next time I'm in a jam," Kayla suggests, and Jax's laugh echoes down the long hall that keeps swaying. I feel like I'm walking on a balance beam.

"You're *always* in a jam because you're never where you say you are," Jax says.

"True," Kayla says with a sigh.

"Where do you always sneak off to anyway?" Jax asks.

Kayla smiles mischievously. "A good crook never reveals her secrets. You should know that."

"Former crook! Former crook!" Jax repeats as if he's reading from one of the many self-help textbooks I found in our dorm room with titles like *Three Steps to Good* and *Sinister to Sweet.*

Bells chime to announce that class is starting, and I cover my ears because they're so loud. They're probably deafening to keep anyone from using the famous lateness excuse: "I didn't hear the bell." Well, I did, and I am about to get my first tardy.

"I should get to troll hunting before the classroom door evaporates." Jax winks at us, then hands Kayla the handkerchief in his shirt pocket. "Have fun in therapy, girls."

Kayla groans. "Of all the classes for you to have first, the Evil Queen's class is the worst." Kayla clutches her stomach. "Professor Harlow makes you talk about your feelings and makes kids cry. She's evil."

"Maybe that's why she's called the Evil Queen," I say breezily as we hurry into the classroom, dodging shifting castle walls. I dive through a door that is bricking itself shut and throw my butt into the seat closest to the exit. "How mean can a therapy teacher really be?"

"Pretty mean," Kayla whispers as she runs past me to a seat in the back. "Don't say anything about—"

"Miss Gillian Cobbler, how nice of you to grace us with your presence this morning," I hear someone interrupt in a voice that practically purrs.

The Evil Queen is definitely intimidating. I'll give her that right off the bat. She's much taller than I imagined—even taller with that elaborate feather-and-crystal headpiece—and her clothes are stunning. (She's wearing a plush-green velvet gown with silver crystals around her tiny waist.) Her looks could rival the princesses' if not for her sourpuss expression and long, pale face that makeup does nothing to hide. Harlow's elaborately beaded gown drags along the cobblestone floor of the drafty room as she walks toward me.

"Do you think just because you're new, you can get away with being late?" She purses her lavender lips and leans on my desk, drumming her purple nails. Her eyes are as dark as coal.

I try not to sound nervous. "No, but you could go a little easy on me. You need a map to get around this place."

I'm expecting someone to laugh—like they would in my trade-school classes—but the rest of the class is so quiet you could hear a pin drop.

"Is that supposed to be funny? Therapy isn't funny." The Evil Queen snaps her fingers, and my name shows up on the board behind her desk. The word "tardy" appears. "Your first tardy in your first class! Well done, cobbler's daughter!" She applauds halfheartedly, and the crow on her shoulder squawks in agreement. "I can see you're another fine feather in the cap of our school."

Behind me, I hear someone snort. "What do you expect from someone whose dad makes cheap shoes for a living?"

I whip around. No one insults my family. The girl behind me is dressed in black from head to toe. She's wearing a skirt covered in a strange pattern of moons and stars. Why doesn't she have to wear a uniform? "Excuse me?"

"You heard me," she says coolly, her jet-black eyes staring right through me. "Think you can do something about it? A lowly cobbler's daughter?"

I'm thunderstruck. The Evil Queen may seem evil, but is she really going to let this girl talk to me like that? I look around for allies.

This is the first chance I've had to size everyone up. Trade school was mostly made up of humans and your occasional troll. Here I see students who are ogres, goblins, mermaids, fairies, gnomes, and magical creatures I've only read about in storybooks. There are even desks in giant fish tanks! Two mermaids zapped into them while this girl was being rude to me. Other than her, the mermaids are the only two not forced to wear these itchy navy uniforms.

"For starters, I can deck you hard enough to knock you out of your chair," I say, anger bubbling up inside me. I rise from my chair. "That should keep you from insulting people you don't even know."

I hear a high-pitched laugh and then feel long fingers digging into my shoulder. "Sit down, Miss Cobbler, before I send you to detention. First a tardy, and now you're threatening my sister?"

This girl is the Evil Queen's sister? If Harlow's sister is in FTRS too, she must be really bad news.

My professor tsks. "You certainly want to get on my bad side, don't you? I'm not sure that's wise." She snaps her fingers, and behind her the board starts to write more notes. "Gillian Cobbler—Anger issues, problems with authority, threatening other students. Recommend extended stay." My heart plummets. Professor Harlow leans close to my face. She smells like roses. "Do you two need to take this outside?" she asks. "I'm fond of students working out their issues with a little fencing. After all, I do coach the team, and my sister, Jocelyn, is our star fencer."

Fencing was one of the after-school clubs I actually wanted to try out for—before I knew the Evil Queen was the coach. I've only practiced fencing with our fireplace poker, but Mother said I have a knack. Looking at Jocelyn, I'm not sure having a knack is enough, and the last thing I want are problems that will keep me at FTRS longer. As much as it kills me, I can't help but sigh. "No."

"Smart choice," Professor Harlow coos.

Jocelyn leans forward so that her hot breath is on my neck. "You better watch yourself, cobbler's daughter," she whispers. "People who cross my family don't live to tell the tale. Or haven't you heard what we can do with an apple?" I turn around to shoot her a nasty look, and Jocelyn smiles evilly.

"Since this is your first group session, Miss Cobbler, maybe you'd like to share how you wound up at FTRS." Harlow moves back to her desk and takes a seat. I notice a clear glass case with a tiny gold mirror inside. *What's so special about that thing that it needs to be locked away*? I wonder—and I feel a chill when I realize Harlow's eyes are on me. I look away at a large crystal bowl on her desk. Almost every student dutifully brought the Evil Queen a bright red or green apple that looks as if it has been polished with shoe lacquer. I didn't bring one, which is probably another sore spot.

"Umm..." There is no way I'm sharing anything in here.

"Umm?" Professor Harlow mocks in a high-pitched voice. "*Umm*? Is that all you have to say for yourself?" She drums her fingernails on the crystals on her sleeves. "How proud your parents must be of your remarkable intelligence."

A few people laugh. Jocelyn is the loudest.

My eyes narrow, even though I know they shouldn't. "I said 'umm' because there really isn't anything I want to share." *Weakness is not a characteristic you want to share with the world*, I can hear Father say.

Harlow snaps her fingers, and I feel a cold swirling sensation come over me. The room is suddenly windy, and my hair blows in front of my eyes, preventing me from seeing what is happening. Then just as suddenly, the wind dies away, and our desks have been arranged in a circle. It must be time for group sharing. My classmates look somber, and it's easy to see why. From the windowless walls and numerous torches that cast eerie shadows on the wall to the black bird perched on Professor Harlow's shoulder, the vibe is sort of creepy. How is this a room for bonding?

"Maybe a casual group setting will make you more eager to fess up." Harlow appears in front of my desk again as if by magic. No one can move that fast. "Share, Miss Cobbler. *Now*," she says sharply.

I open my mouth, knowing another obnoxious comment will just land me in hotter water, but a short, stocky troll girl beats me to the punch. "I don't mind going first," she says. I smile at her gratefully.

Harlow whirls around, her cape flying in the air behind her like it's going to give her wings. "Then *go*."

"Hi, everyone. I'm Maxine." She tugs on one of her large ears, which are covered in earrings of every gem and stone found in the Enchantasia mines.

"Hi, Maxine," we all say like we're supposed to.

"I've been thinking a lot about the Troll War. Maybe because I lived through it," she says softly. I watch as one of her eyes goes down as she speaks while the other stays in place. "The things I saw still keep me up at night."

"You're a troll," Jocelyn pipes up. "You're supposed to be up at night lurking around." A girl next to her snickers, and I give them both the evil eye.

"Jocelyn," Harlow says in a light tone. "Let her finish. And no name-calling," she adds. "That's my job. Go on, Maxine."

"I keep wondering when the war will finally be over." Maxine side-eyes Jocelyn, one eye rolling in its socket. "When no more lives will be lost."

"Never!" Jocelyn jumps in. "We should let trolls and goblins all kill each other. Who needs either of them?"

Poor Maxine looks like she's going to cry, and I snap. Who does Jocelyn think she is? "We could say the same thing about your family," I speak up. "A lot of people think the Evil Queen should have been banished after what she did to Snow White. Who wants your family in Enchantasia either?"

Jocelyn stares at me darkly, and I feel a deep pinch sink into my right arm.

"Ouch!" How'd she do that?

"Temper, temper, Miss Gillian," Professor Harlow tsks, but she sounds pleased. "You wouldn't want me to give you your first detention for telling lies, would you? Excellent sharing, Jocelyn." Jocelyn smiles smugly, and I roll my eyes.

Squawk! Aldo the crow swoops in and lands on my desk. *Squawk!* It's like he's reporting me for eye-rolling, which is just plain insane, and yet…

Professor Harlow puts out her hand, and Aldo flies back onto her shoulder. The two stare at me disapprovingly. Harlow's eyes travel down to my lace-up boots. "What are those?" she asks. "Those shoes are not proper uniform attire. Surely, the shoemaker's daughter can afford *shoes* at least."

"They hurt my feet," I say. *And they're ugly.*

Harlow snaps her fingers, and my favorite boots are gone and the ugly black school shoes are on my feet. What the…? "Too bad. You can have your old boots back when you learn how to fly like Aldo. Now, Miss Maxine, let's talk about being a troll. Do you feel ashamed to be such a creature?"

"What?" Maxine cries. "That's such a mean thing to say, Professor."

"I was just joking, darling," the Evil Queen says. "I wanted to see where your emotions were, and now we know, don't we? You're ashamed of being a troll."

Thump.

We all look up. I'm thankful for the distraction.

Thump. Thump. Thump.

Professor Harlow looks up at the ceiling in annoyance, but ignores the sounds. "Maxine, tell me your darkest moment being a troll." Her eyes flash green. "Actually, why don't you all recall your darkest moment in a thousand-word essay that must be finished before the end of the class. Start now." She snaps her fingers, and the torches brighten. She uses the opportunity to go to the mirror behind her desk. I watch her examine her face and then reach for one of the purple bottles on her desk. She begins applying lotion to her cheeks.

Thump! Thump! Thump! THUMP Thump! Thump!

The Evil Queen's hand slips, and lotion gets all over the bodice of her dress. She emits a low growl. "What is that racket? *Miri!*" she yells. Aldo flies off Professor Harlow's shoulder and dives over people's heads. "*Miri! Where are you?*"

The mirror in front of Harlow begins to glow green, then orange, then purple. "Harlow, we've been over this," a voice inside the mirror says with a sigh. "Only Headmistress Flora can demand my appearance."

"Well, I'm demanding it anyway," Professor Harlow

seethes. "What is that god-awful noise interrupting my group's therapy session?"

"I'm surprised you haven't dismissed class already," Miri says, sounding anything but nervous at Harlow's tone. "Didn't you get the memo from Flora this morning?"

"What memo?" Harlow yells over the continuing banging, which only seems to grow louder by the minute. Harlow's head whips around to the class. "*Write!*"

We all look down at our papers. I grab a quill and my ink.

"Psst." I look over at Maxine. She offers me a quill. "Use this."

I hold mine up. "Thanks, but mine works fine."

"Oops!" I hear Miri sing. "I was supposed to give you the memo. Just like you were supposed to tell me about the meeting in Flora's office yesterday."

Maxine shakes her head, and her lazy eye does a quick bounce. Her thick-rimmed glasses match the color of her light-brown hair. "Use this. There's a message in it from a friend." She passes the quill over as Harlow and Miri argue. "Write with it. You'll see."

What does she mean the quill has a message in it? I look at it, wondering if there is a secret compartment, but I don't see one. I dip the quill in the ink, and nothing happens. Then I try putting the quill to paper. That's when things get weird. I know what I want to write, but instead, different words come out.

Hey, G! It's me! K! Cool quill, huh? Sorry I didn't warn you about Jocelyn. I'm not feeling great. Going to skip the next class and lie down for a while. Can you give me some peace and quiet? I'll give you the grand tour of FTRS later! I promise!

After the words appear, the ink slowly disappears again, leaving a blank page.

That. Is. So. Cool. I write her back.

Feel better! We'll hang out later. –G

The words appear then disappear. Amazing. "Psst." I pass Maxine the quill. She grabs it when Harlow isn't looking.

"I have never seen this memo before!" Harlow is yelling. "Flora canceled today's classes to paint the castle? That's ridiculous!"

"What's ridiculous is that we haven't done it already," Miri tells her. "The princesses have agreed to Royal Day happening in less than two weeks, and there is a lot to prepare before their arrival."

"I'm not canceling classes for a paint session!" Harlow says incredulously. "They'll have to paint around us!"

We put our heads back down to write, but the banging only gets louder. It's hard to concentrate. I see the mer-boy's water quill fly out of his hand at the hammering, which must be amplified in his tank. Then there is a knock at the door.

"'Scuse me, ma'am?" A peasant in paint-splattered clothes and a cap stands in the doorway with a brush and a bucket. The smell of the paint hits my nose almost instantly. "We need to get started in this room." He looks around. "Wow, Murray, get in here," he calls to someone. "This room is the worst yet!"

I hear Miri muffle a laugh.

"Do you mind?" Harlow says, and with a flick of her wrist, the door slams in the peasant's face. She sighs. "Children, it seems that our time together needs to come to an end."

A small cheer is quickly extinguished as Aldo nosedives at the boy who is the loudest.

"*But*," Professor Harlow says, letting the word linger in the air, "I expect this paper on my desk tomorrow." Everyone groans. "Enjoy your afternoon, class." She opens the door again, and Murray enters slowly.

I gather my things and think about how I'm going to use my time now that there is no class and I can't go back to our room. I guess I could practice fencing near the woods. Sounds like I'll be dueling Jocelyn in our classroom soon enough.

"Hi, Gilly." Maxine is waiting for me. "Thanks for sticking up for me back there. No one ever does that." She looks down at her huge shoes. Father would have a hard time making boots for those clonkers.

"That's what friends are for," I say automatically. Maybe Miri will notice and mark me down for good behavior. Maxine's smile widens. Her teeth are a little green.

"Are you doing anything right now?" Maxine asks. "Want me to show you around? I mean, I'm sure you have loads of people who want to show you around, but I would if you wanted. I've been here a year, so I know every room in the joint."

I want to work the "So what are you in for?" question into our conversation, but I can't figure out how to do it without offending her. For some reason, I suspect it has something to do with jewelry. She's wearing at least a half a dozen shiny necklaces.

Jocelyn walks by Maxine with a friend and whispers something. The two burst out laughing, and Maxine looks down, embarrassed.

"I mean, if you don't mind being seen with me." Maxine's eye droops again.

I stare defiantly at Jocelyn. There's nothing I hate more than bullies (and royals, but bullies more so). "Of course I want to hang out with you. Let's go." I brush past Jocelyn, taking Maxine by the hand. "Any suggestions on what to do?"

The two of us leave the dungeon-classroom behind, and the light shining through the hallway windows makes me feel brighter. Painters are painting the trim along the windows while cleaners wipe down the statues and gargoyles. A tarp is being hung in the central hallway that says "Fairy Tale Reform School" in large, gold script. Fresh flowers are in vases everywhere I look. Anna would love all this preparation for the princesses. I know it's only been a day, but I thought she'd write right away.

"Have you tried Pegasus flying yet?" Maxine asks. "There's free time right now."

I've never flown before. Now is as good a time as any to start. A paper for the Evil Queen can definitely wait. I smile. "That sounds up my alley. Let's go."

CHAPTER 7

Flying Lessons

Thanks to a new hallway that appears when we leave class, we make it to the stables in no time.

"You guys here for a ride?" asks a stable boy who's raking hay. "I'll tell you what I told the girl that just left—the woods are off-limits to students and Pegasi. The last thing we need is to lose another Pegasus to a giant. Pegasi are their favorite snack."

Eww.

"Should I suit up two beauties for you?" The boy heads to the stalls. I can hear the Pegasi munching on hay and neighing. I've never been this close to them before—other than the time I snuck into the stables in the village to steal a gold harness some foolish stable boy left hanging on a wall.

"You've got an hour 'til the Royal Ladies-in-Waiting Club comes for their afternoon fly over the princesses' castle."

Double *eww*. I read about this school club. Their sole purpose is to dote on the princesses. No thank you!

"Yes, we'd like a ride," I say, getting excited.

He looks at me skeptically. "You're new here. You've ridden before, right?"

"Of course," I lie. I mean, how hard can it be?

The boy heads off to grab me some gear.

"Gilly? I think I've changed my mind about the flying." Maxine sounds jittery. Her good eye stares at the stalls. "I was trying to impress you by asking, but to be honest, when I get in the air, I feel dizzy. It's hard to fly with just one good eye." Her bad one spins in its socket.

Poor girl. "It's okay," I say, trying not to sound disappointed. I can't just ditch her. Can I? "We can do something else."

Maxine twirls her green gem necklace. "No, you go! You can tell me about your flight at dinner. I could sit at your table. I mean, if you have room?" she asks hopefully.

I smile. "Of course, there's room. I'll see you tonight."

Maxine heads off, leaving me alone to explore the gleaming white-and-gold stables. Photos of students in the

Pegasus Flying Club at championship races line the walls near the entrance, along with various ribbons and trophies in a shiny, silver case. Beyond me are the stalls and gear, which are much nicer than at the dwarf squad stables. (I've, um, seen those a few times when I've been hauled in.) Those stables have a roof, but the Pegasus stables don't. When I look up, I can see Pegasi flying high above, never veering far from sight.

"If you don't have a roof, how do you keep the Pegasi from flying away?" I ask as the stable boy comes back with two helmets and saddles.

"Magic," he says, looking at me like this should be obvious. "The roof closes at night, but during the day, we like these beauties to have their freedom when they're not needed for lessons." He hands me a helmet. "This should fit. Hey, where's your friend?"

"She bailed," I say.

The stable boy sighs. "I already told Mighty and Macho you were taking them."

I laugh. "Like they understand you!"

He doesn't look amused. "Of course they do! Pegasi can't talk, but they can understand human thoughts. You should know that if you've ridden before." He takes the helmet from me suspiciously, and I start to protest.

"I'll go up with her."

I turn around. Jax is leaning on the open stable doors.

"What are you doing here?" I ask him.

Jax takes the helmet from the boy and hands it back to me. "I ran into Maxine, and she said where you were." He grins mischievously. "So you're an expert Pegasus flyer, huh?"

I jut out my chin. "Is that so hard to believe?"

"Yes," the stable boy and Jax say at the same time.

"I'll take Mighty, and she can take Macho," Jax tells the boy. "She'll be fine with me." The stable boy nods and heads to the stalls.

Jax motions for me to join them, but suddenly my feet don't want to comply. Flying sounded like a good idea 'til I was actually about to do it. I don't know how to hold the reins or what to say to a Pegasus to give directions! What if I fall off? I'll wind up as flat as a gingerbread man.

Jax takes my arm. "Relax. You can't imagine how easy this is. And the rush of being in the sky and seeing the freedom outside these walls can't be beat."

The stable boy opens a large stall, and I hear neighs.

"Mighty and Macho, they're ready for you. These boys are twins," he tells me.

I peek my head inside and inhale sharply. The Pegasi are majestic. And huge. Their white coats practically glow, they're so bright, and their wings are nearly double the size of their bodies, even if they are currently folded down at their sides. The Pegasi neigh softly as we approach.

The stable boy pets the bridge of their noses. "Hop on. They'll take you up and around the grounds."

I watch Jax stick his foot in the foothold and easily pull himself up. I walk over to Macho. "Hey, boy," I say softly. "Think you can help me out? I'm not that good at this." The Pegasus blinks his bright blue eyes and nudges me as if to say "no problem." I do like Jax does and am amazed when I'm able to pull myself right up. Awesome.

"Keep an eye on the time," the stable boy tells us, pointing to the clock on the Pegasus's harness. "*Don't* leave the grounds since you aren't with an instructor—or you'll get detention—and *don't* go into the Hollow Woods." He says sharply, "Got it?"

"Got it," we say, and then without warning, the Pegasi's wings begin to expand and we're rising slowly out of the stables and into the sky. My stomach feels like it might fall out as the stable below gets farther and farther away. The wind begins to blow my hair away from my face, and I hold on to the reins tightly as the Pegasus begins to flap its wings faster and takes me high above the grounds.

I'm flying!

I start to laugh out of both fear and excitement. I've never been on a Pegasus before. In the village, they were always for the rich or the royals, and yet here at FTRS, flying is a regular privilege. I have to admit, it's a pretty nice student perk to have.

"Just hang on. I'll tell them where to go," Jax says as his Pegasus flaps next to mine.

I look down and see we're over the school now. Below, I can make out students on the lawns fencing or playing dodgeball or just lounging on the grass. I'm afraid to turn my head, but I do, ever so slightly, and can just make out the village of Enchantasia in the distance. I'd give anything to fly over my boot right now and talk to my siblings, but I don't want to extend my stay at FTRS any longer than I have to. In the opposite direction, the Hollow Woods loom darkly.

Jax pulls alongside me, looking completely at ease. I'm

still fighting the urge to close my eyes. "Pretty cool, huh?" he says.

"You do this often?" I clutch Macho's reins tighter.

"Often enough." Jax uses only one hand to hold the reins. With the other, he pets Mighty's head. "So where do you want to go?" He gets a mischievous glint in his eyes. "I know! We should have brought water balloons to drop on Jocelyn."

"Maxine told you what happened in class?" We're flying over the castle now, and I can't help staring at the beautiful turrets and stone statues that sit atop each peak. I believe they're gargoyles. Sensing my curiosity, Macho brings me closer. We fly by two ugly gray ones with nasty faces, and I can't believe how long their claws are.

Macho bucks slightly, and I hold on tighter. "It's okay, boy. They're just statues," I say, knowing he can understand me. He begins to pull away. I glance back at the creepy gargoyles one last time and…huh. That's funny. I could have sworn the gargoyles' heads were turned the other way—but that's impossible.

"Jax, those gargoyles aren't real, are they?" I ask as Macho catches up to him.

Jax laughs. "You've been reading too many fairy tales, Cobbler."

It must have been my imagination. Then my eyes spot something lying on a flat roof. "My boots!" I will Macho to head back to the roof, and Jax follows. "Harlow zapped them off my feet during class and said I'd only find them when I could fly."

"You've got good eyes," Jax says, landing on the roof first and picking up the boots. I dismount from Macho and change my shoes, lacing up my boots quickly. *Ahhh.* That's so much better. I stick the uniform ones in the satchel on Macho's side. "So where do you want to fly to next?" Jax asks. "Any chance you want to see the woods?"

"I thought we weren't allowed near them."

"We're not—technically—but we can fly close enough," Jax says casually. "Might be your only chance to see a giant up close." I don't say anything. "Unless you're too scared to go. I wouldn't blame you. My roommate, Ollie, says when he was playing rugby out in the fields the other day, he saw smoke coming from the woods." He shrugs.

I touch Macho. I don't want him getting eaten. He neighs softly. "Then maybe we should avoid that area. Not that I'm scared."

Jax gives me a look. "Liar! I can tell you're lying because when you do, your nose scrunches up like a little rat."

"I'm not scared!" I insist and jump on Macho again. "I just don't see the need to get detention. It's not like we're going to see anything wicked going on in a flyby over the woods anyway."

Macho startles me by taking off at top speed.

"Slow down," I say as clouds blur by and the wind feels as cold as snow. "Slow down!" Macho ignores me and keeps racing. I can hear Jax behind us yelling, but between the wind and the low cloud cover, I can't see or hear him. What am I going to do? My heart is racing. Visions of falling off pop into my mind. I hold on as he climbs higher above the clouds, where it's so bright that I have to squint. Just when I think Macho has lost his mind, he dives and I actually scream at the speed we're going. When he slows down, I realize we're high above some dark green treetops. We're at the edge of the Hollow Woods.

"Thank you for stopping, but why would you bring me somewhere you could get eaten?" I wait for my heartbeat to slow down.

"If you wanted to race, you could have just said so," Jax scolds me when he finally catches up. "You could have been killed. You need to—"

"Talk to my Pegasus," I say. "I did. He wouldn't listen."

"Pegasi always listen," Jax says as if he doesn't believe me.

"Well, mine didn't and—hey, is that Headmistress Flora?" I point to a tiny figure in a robe that is walking quickly to the edge of the supposedly dangerous and spooky woods. The black-and-white-speckled hair and prim clothes definitely remind me of the woman I met yesterday. "What would she being doing out here?"

"That can't be her." Jax frowns. "She never leaves her office."

"Oh, it's her all right," I say as she looks around—but not up—and then slips in between the trees. I feel my heart speed up like it's a drum.

Gotcha.

If my headmistress is keeping secrets, I'm going to find out what they are. Maybe dirt on her is my early ticket to freedom.

Chapter 8

Sweet Dreams

As soon as the key turns in my dorm-room door, my eyes fly open. Mother says I have the hearing of a bat.

I lie motionless as the door opens and Kayla tiptoes inside, choosing not to turn on the light and wake me up. Then she bangs into a coatrack.

"*Ouch! Ouch!*" Kayla yells at the top of her lungs. "*Yowza!*"

I turn on the oil lamp at the side of my bed and see Kayla hopping around on one foot. She's still wearing our navy uniform, even though school has been over for hours. I am surprised she doesn't change out of them as soon as classes are over. I do. Her wings shoot out, and soon she's fluttering up and down, holding her aching toe.

"You okay?" I ask.

She holds her breath, then lets it go. "Sorry, roomie. I was trying not to wake you."

This is the first time I've seen Kayla in our room since I arrived a few days ago. I was starting to think I lived alone. Not that I mind. I almost never had a room to myself for more than thirty seconds in our boot.

Kayla flutters to her bed and sits across from me. She makes a face. "Sorry we still haven't gone on a proper tour of FTRS."

"It's okay." I sit up, pushing my heavy quilt from home off me. "I've been exploring on my own." *It's the perfect excuse to watch ol' Flora and see if there is anything I can use to get out of here.*

"I didn't even help you move in." Kayla sounds like she feels bad.

I shrug. "I really didn't have much to unpack." This quilt Mother made me when I was a baby, a few pieces of clothing, and a family drawing are all the possessions I own. Kayla looks like she's moved in permanently.

The stone walls in our round room are decorated with colorful designs that Kayla painted, and silver streamers with tiny gold stars hang from our ceiling. They make me feel like we're at a royal ball rather than in a bedroom. Ours is almost at the tip of the turret in the girls' dormitories. (They keep trolls near the bottom level so they can't snap and accidentally destroy the place.) Just getting to the room is a workout (twenty-four floors), but it seems worth the price. My boot was tiny and crowded, and someone was always crying or needing a diaper change. When I walk through this door, the room is mine and mine alone. Well, mine and Kayla's.

"It's a pretty good room," Kayla says, seeming to read my thoughts as her legs swing off the side of her bed. "I feel safe when I'm in here," she says softly. "Sometimes I almost think I'm better off staying in here permanently." I look at her strangely. Kayla holds out a mini magical scroll. I can't believe she owns something so pricy. I wonder if she stole it. "Did you see today's headline?" She pulls the scroll away. "I almost don't want to show it to you. It might give you nightmares."

I roll my eyes. "You sound like the Wicked Stepmother."

"*Former*," Kayla teases. "But seriously. Enchantasia is not as safe as everyone thinks it is."

Underneath the purple calligraphy and hearts, castles, and flowers that adorn every headline on *Happily Ever After Scrolls* is a much darker story.

Gottie Spotted in Rowland. Harking Family Missing.

"Mr. Harking has been tracking Gottie for the last two years," Kayla says, explaining the article before I even read it. "I heard Wolfington talking about him once. I think Mr. Harking worked for the school. Now he and his whole family have disappeared." Her eyes are as big as the moon. "Just for *looking*."

I feel suddenly cold—and not because castles are drafty. I think of Mother, Father, Anna, Han, Hamish, Felix, and Trixie being taken away because of my spying, and my stomach begins to churn. "I'm sure someone will catch her eventually. Flora said they were trying to bring her in."

"*Trying*," Kayla repeated. "I don't think anyone is ever going to catch her." Kayla floats to her dresser, snaps her fingers, and *POOF!* she's wearing shimmery blue pj's. She looks at the picture of my family that Father had a fairyographer whip up for Mother's birthday. It's of my whole clan in front of our boot. Mother packed it with my things. "You're lucky you have such a great family."

I go to my dresser and look at the picture too. I'm wearing faded green pajamas. They pale in comparison to Kayla's. "Yeah, they're keepers," I say, ignoring the look of Father in the picture. His mouth is curved down in a deep frown. "Do you have a picture of your family?"

Kayla's eyes flash, and immediately I wonder how I've said the wrong thing.

"I don't have a family," she says flatly. "Rumpelstiltskin took them from me."

"What?" I try to understand. "Why would Rumpelstiltskin want your family?" Just saying his name out loud sends shivers down my spine. His name rolled off Kayla's tongue like she's said it a thousand times before.

Kayla's button nose scrunches tight. "He doesn't need a reason!" she snaps. "Sorry. It's a touchy subject." She stares out our tiny, stained glass window into the moonlight. "The last time I saw them was the day before I left for FTRS," she says quietly. "Mother asked me to go to the village to get rolls for my last dinner at home. She said the dinner was to celebrate the beginning of my new life." Kayla rolls her eyes. "I hated her for saying that. I told her FTRS was her way of trying to get rid of me, and she denied it." Kayla looks down at her nails, which have sparkly blue polish on them.

"We had a huge fight, and when I came back, she was gone." Her voice is hollow. "She, my sisters, the hollow tree we lived in, the garden where we grew turnips. Gone. As if none of it—or us—ever existed." Kayla slumps against the wall 'til she looks like a crumpled dress on the floor. "When I tried to find them, a peddler told me he saw Rumpelstiltskin make them disappear."

I'm too stunned to speak. I sit down next to Kayla, waiting for her to cry. She doesn't. I'm not a big hugger, but at a moment like this, it seems appropriate. I awkwardly put an arm around her and squeeze. "I'm so sorry." I mean it.

"Thanks." Kayla pulls away from me and traces a yellow starburst on the wall with her finger. I have a feeling she painted it. "It's been three years now."

Three years without a family. Without a home. How did she survive? "You've been here that long?" No wonder this room looks so lived in.

"I was on my own for a while." Kayla's face has an eerie glow in the low light. "I tried to find them, and to survive, I sold illegal goods like the fake handbags I'm always selling to Flora's foolish daughters, Azalea and Dahlia. Eventually the dwarf police caught up with me and sent me here."

Hearing Kayla's story makes me want to write to Anna. I wonder if she's doing okay without me. Do she, Trixie, Han, Hamish, and Felix have enough to eat? How could I have let myself get caught and mess up their only chance at having a decent meal every night? Han is probably so hungry that he's crying. I'm so mad at myself. I—

"Do you hear violins?" I ask.

Kayla groans. "Yes. I should have warned you." She quickly stands up. "Our downstairs neighbors, Eunice and Beatrice, like to practice their violins at bedtime."

I listen to them play. "They're pretty good."

Kayla gives me a look. "You say that now, but you won't in a few days." She stomps on the floor loudly. I join in. "Keep it down!" The music stops, and we high-five. Thankfully, Kayla is smiling again. Our conversation about her family is seemingly forgotten.

Then the violins start again. They're louder.

Kayla growls. "They wouldn't!" Her wings appear almost instantly.

I wince as Eunice—or Beatrice—begins to play off-key. I'm not sure if it's on purpose. "They're making a stand."

"Well, we're not going to let them get away with it." Kayla grabs her wand and grins mischievously. "Miri has to be asleep. So how do you feel about a little dance party?" She flicks her wand, and loud music fills our room.

I grab Kayla's hand and stomp away, the two of us spinning in a circle 'til all my worries disappear.

Pegasus Postal Service
Flying Letters Since The Troll War!

FROM: Gillian Cobbler (Fairy Tale Reform School*)

*Letter checked for suspicious content

TO: Anna Cobbler (2 Boot Way)

Dear Anna Banana,

I guess you've figured out by now that I'm going to be here awhile. I'm so sorry I messed up your birthday. I just want you to have everything I don't, but I promise I'll figure out a better way to do that than swiping from royals. I've only been here a few days, but FTRS doesn't seem that bad so far. For the first time ever, I sort of have my own room. You'd love the dorm. You get your own bed, and no one leaves smelly socks on the floor. I can picture you hanging up one of your Rapunzel ads and putting Grandma's mirror on your dresser. (Yes, we have dressers! Not sacks hanging from the wall with all our clothes.)

If this wasn't a reform school, I'd send for you immediately. I do have some good news: Headmistress Flora says if I behave, you guys can come for the anniversary ball. Take care of the family for me. And watch Han and Hamish around that new shoe polish Mother made. It may smell like gum, but trust me, it doesn't taste like it.

Love, Gilly

Happily Ever After Scrolls

Brought to you by FairyWeb—magically appearing on scrolls throughout Enchantasia for the past ten years!

Meet the Wolf Man!*

by Beatrice Beez

Name: Xavier Wolfington (formerly known as "the Wolf")

Occupation: Professor of history at Fairy Tale Reform School

Hobbies: Meditation, yoga, and putting the pedal to the metal in spin class at Hansel and Gretel's Power Gym

Strengths: Lightning fast on two or four feet, keen sense of smell, bronze medal in the Enchantasia Olympics for long jump

Weakness: Silver bullets

Likes: Peace and quiet, reading history books. Rumored to be writing a book on the psychological effects of the Troll War

Dislikes: Talk of his former life (Never *ever* mention Granny!)

Still a mystery: Where he disappears every full moon

Love life: There was that rumored romance with a fairy, but as far as we know, Professor Wolfington is currently single

**Xavier Wolfington declined to be interviewed for this story. All opinions expressed in this story are Happily Ever After Scrolls' own.*

CHAPTER 9

You've Been Schooled

Good morning, class."

"Good morning, Professor Wolfington," the entire class says in unison.

I can't help staring at my history professor—and not just because he's a wolf man who could eat me for breakfast. I still can't get the image out of my head of what happened last week. Professor Wolfington *leaped* two whole stories to stop Jax. I tend to avoid people who could kill me with one furry paw—I mean, hand! I can see the Wolf's forearms bulging through his ruffled dress shirt right now. He must work out.

"Since our three-part assembly 'Magic: The Good and Evil of It' took the place of our last class, I haven't heard about your weekend." Wolfington walks around the classroom. "What did you all do?"

A teacher caring about our lives outside of class? Wow, this place is different.

This classroom is the prettiest one I have class in. No creepy gargoyles staring at me while I fumble for an answer. This room reminds me of a church with its stained glass floor-to-ceiling windows showing famous moments in Enchantasia history. There's one of Ella's wedding, one of Rose awakening from her slumber, and a picture of Rapunzel in her tower. I could stare at those windows for hours…and at those brass rings holding back the velvet drapes. If those babies are real, I could fetch a pretty penny for them at Arabian Nights Pawn Shop.

"I had a really nice weekend, Professor!" says Maxine. She's so much larger than many of my classmates that her knees barely fit under her desk. "My friends and I had a picnic near the remains of Galmour Castle."

"Like you have any friends," I hear Jocelyn mumble from across the classroom.

That witch really gets under my skin.

"Excellent, Miss Maxine!" Wolfington says. "Anyone else?"

A pretty raven-haired mermaid in a fish tank holds up a mirror. I watch as words magically appear on it. It says: "Went deep-sea fishing and found where Prince Harrison's ship wrecked. I am going to write my next report on him."

"Good, Miss Clara!" Professor Wolfington says approvingly. "If you want to write an essay for extra credit, you can. I won't be assigning another paper for two weeks."

A pixie sitting on an oversized desk glares at Clara. She's had her hand up for a while, but I'm not sure Professor Wolfington saw it. Her hand is pretty tiny.

"I went canoeing down Quarry Cannon," says a gnome in a pointy hat that has funny fake ogre ears glued to the sides. "That guidebook you gave me was awesome. Who knew how many sites were left over from the Troll War?"

Why is everyone here kissing up to the Wolf? Are they that scared of being eaten? Or do they genuinely like the guy?

"Good, Mr. Helmut," our professor says as he strolls row to row. "Finding something that helps you mellow out is an important tool—and look at all you learned at the same time. We all need anchors." Another hand shoots up, and Wolfington smirks. "Ah, Mr. Ollie. What wisdom would you like to share with the class today?"

"I have more of a question than an announcement of an extra-credit kiss-up paper," says Ollie, who happens to be Jax's roommate. Short and stocky, with dark skin he says he got from so many days on the high sea (rumor is he was a stowaway on a pirate ship), what Ollie lacks in height he makes up for in friendliness and storytelling. Jax says he's really good at magic tricks. ("It's how he landed in this place," Jax says. "He was always making people's things disappear into his pocket.")

"When you say anchors, do you mean metaphorical anchors or actual anchors that we can haul around as good luck charms?" Ollie asks. Half the class groans. "Anchors are pretty heavy."

Before Wolfington can answer, Miri's mirror starts to make noise and glow. I notice everyone in the class sit up straighter.

Beep! Beep! Beep!

"Sorry to interrupt, Professor." Miri's voice comes through loud and clear. "The headmistress needs to see Helmut immediately."

The gnome's face drops. "I didn't do it."

"Do what?" Wolfington asks calmly.

"Break into the cafeteria last night and eat two apple

cream pies," the gnome says. The follow-up burp doesn't help his case.

"Funny, I see things differently," Miri chirps. The mirror begins to glow a rainbow of colors, and then an image fills the screen. It's Helmut clearly picking the lock to the kitchen, and yep, there he is digging into a pie. He's a fast eater. Helmut hangs his head.

Whoa. Miri is such a tattletale.

Helmut sighs and grabs his books. "Sorry, Professor Wolfington."

Wolfington straightens Helmut's hat on the way out. "Good luck, Helmut. So, anchors. I mean figurative ones, Ollie." Ollie nods, and Wolfington stops at Jax's desk. "How about you, Mr. Jax. How was your weekend?"

Jax mumbles something and then goes back to doodling in his notebook. I wonder if Wolfington bought my story about Jax trying to sneak outside to get my notebook my first day here. Somehow, I don't think you can pull one over on the wolf man like you can on mousy Professor Grimes from our recent assembly, "Your Life, Your Career in Enchantasia: How to Find a Noble Profession That Is *Legal*." She let half the school go to the bathroom at the same time! They never came back to the great hall to hear the rest of the lecture.

"Isn't that correct, Miss Gillian?"

Fiddlesticks. Wolfington is speaking to me now, isn't he? What would a wolf man ask me the first five minutes of class? "Yes, I'm sleeping great. The pillows here are fantastic."

"Pay attention, Cobbler!" Jocelyn says, and someone laughs.

I play with the collar on my white shirt. "Uh, the mattresses are kind of firm, but…" Kayla, who is sitting two rows ahead of me, shakes her head ever so slightly. The professor's blue eyes go right through me. "That wasn't the question, was it?"

Wow, werewolves smile! "I said, you're pretty new to our school having only been here a week, correct?"

"Oh! Yep. Brand spanking new," I say. Jocelyn sighs loudly.

"Well, then, Miss Gillian, maybe you will have a fresh take on what we were studying before all our assemblies this week. Oh, and students, don't forget tomorrow we have another assembly on behavior for Royal Day: 'Finding the Prince and Princess within Yourself.'" Professor Wolfington ignores more groans and goes to the blackboard. A lesson appears on it. "Last week we were discussing how the princesses came to power."

Er...was I placed in the right grade? "My last class was in glass slipper making."

Professor Wolfington sits on the edge of his desk. Through his shirtsleeves I can see a lot of hair. "Take your time." Jocelyn makes a loud clicking sound with her tongue that I assume is supposed to sound like a ticking clock.

"I..." Professor Wolfington waits patiently, but I can picture him running at warp speed toward my desk and hanging me on a hook at the back of the classroom.

"Anyone would be a better ruler than those airheads." We all turn around. My thoughts exactly. I'm surprised to see it's Jax who said that. An ogre pounds his hands on his desk in agreement, and the desk cracks.

"Interesting sentiment, Mr. Jax." Professor Wolfington strokes his beard. "Ruling isn't a popularity contest. It requires tough choices that are right for a whole kingdom. Do you think the princesses are capable of making them?" Jax looks away. "Anyone?"

WOOO-OOH! WOOO-OH! WOOO-OH!

An alarm goes off overhead with such intensity that I have to cover my ears.

Headmistress Flora's voice comes over the intercom.

"Students, this is an evacuation drill." A gnome muffles her cry. Why is she so worked up over a drill? "Report to your assigned stations at once and wait for further instructions."

Professor Wolfington claps his hands. "Okay, students, you heard the headmistress. Go to your assigned stations immediately. Do not panic!"

Some good that instruction does. Everyone in the room begins to freak out. A troll boy is crying. The sea creatures shoot downward out of their tanks. Jocelyn strolls out of the room calmly, while the pixie flies out and leaves her book bag behind. I spin around, unsure of what is happening or where I'm supposed to go. Nobody told me anything about an assigned station. I look desperately for Kayla, but she seems to have disappeared. Why does a drill have everyone in such a tizzy? We had fire drills at trade school all the time. You're used to it when your school has a thatched roof.

"Hey, Jax, what's with the drill?" I start to say, turning to look for him, but he's gone too. *Humph*. Some friends I've made, leaving me to fend for myself in this empty room.

But on second thought…

Miri is probably occupied with everything going on. The Wolf is gone. I look around to make sure no one else is watching, then head to the velvet drapes and slide off two brass rings. What the heck? I'll take two more. The four fit in my two skirt pockets, but they do weigh the pockets down a bit. Who cares? These babies will feed my brothers and sisters for a month. I slip out the classroom door and enter total chaos.

Ogres are running at top speed (for them). Fairies are flying, even though it's against the rules. Two trolls thump by me carrying a desk lamp and a gold trophy. I begin heading toward one exit when the hallway disappears in front of me. A troll next to me starts to cry. "We're trapped!" he says.

"Oh, for Pete's sake, someone tell Miri to shut off the magical hallway mover!" I hear one older girl say to another one. They're dressed in beautiful, matching jade-green dresses, so they're not students, and they seem to be in charge. They're directing students to a new exit that just popped up in a stained glass window. I realize I've seen these girls' pictures in Flora's office. They must be her daughters, Azalea and Dahlia. Kayla said they are student teachers here—and two of her best customers for her fake bag business.

Dahlia puts her hand out in front of a cute boy. "Where are you going, Geoff? You can use my exit if you want instead of going all the way to your station." She giggles girlishly, and I roll my eyes.

"Thanks, Dahlia!" Geoff's voice is sickeningly sweet, like taffy. "That's a nice dress."

Dahlia blushes, and her rosy cheeks turn downright purple. "Oh, this ol' thing? Aren't you sweet!"

"Dahlia!" Azalea yells. "He can't use our exit. He has to go to his station." Geoff sighs. "All of you, get a move on." As everyone moves like cattle to the window to exit, I notice Flora slip down a new hall that just appeared. Why isn't she evacuating?

Ouch! A troll knocks two girls and me down as he pushes past us to get through the window exit first. I shake myself off and get up, but the two girls burst into tears.

"Zeus, geez! Chill!" Azalea reprimands the troll. "We're all leaving, but you…"

That's when I make my break for it.

Too bad I'm so loud. When I run, the brass rings in my pocket clink together, and the sound echoes through the hall. I cringe, thinking Flora will hear me. At the same time, I'm worried she'll get away—which she does. I have to find her.

"What are you doing, sticky fingers?" Jax asks, appearing out of nowhere. He's got his arms folded across his chest like he's just been hanging out, waiting for me to run by him. "You're supposed to be at your evacuation station—and what's that you're hiding?" Jax's violet eyes look disapproving.

I shove the rings deeper in my pockets. "No one told me what my station was."

"It's listed in your welcome pack," Jax says.

"Yeah, I didn't read that," I admit. "What's everyone so worked up about if it's just a drill?"

"Sometimes drills aren't drills here," Jax says. "Last time the alarm went off, someone thought Gottie had gotten onto school grounds. They said she was looking for that Mr. Harking who just went missing. They never found her, but it shook a lot of kids up. Now when they hear drill, they think we're being invaded by evil fairies."

Interesting. I wonder if that's why Flora wasn't evacuating. Is she looking to see if we've had a break-in, or is she *letting* someone break in? Hmm...I could use some good intel to my advantage. Two new hallways pop up behind Jax. I need to get down one of them and find Flora.

"I guess I should get to my evacuation station then." I start to walk away. "See you outside."

"Whoa, whoa, whoa. I see that look in your eye." Jax sizes me up. "You're not going outside. What are you up to?"

"Nothing," I lie, holding my hand on one pocket to keep the brass rings from clinking.

"You can tell me," Jax says, leaning against the door to a room with a sign that says: Archery—Don't lose an eye! Announce yourself before entering. "I'm trustworthy."

I snort. Seeing him standing there in his crisply pressed uniform with a dress shirt underneath his vest instead of the usual tee everyone else is wearing, I don't believe that for a second. He looks too perfect, like he's hiding something. "You still haven't told me why you were trying so hard to escape one minute and then seem perfectly at home here the next. You haven't tried to escape again since I got here," I accuse him.

Jax raises an eyebrow. "How do you know that for sure?"

"I guess I don't, but that doesn't mean I trust you." I sniff. "I've got things to do on my own."

"You sound like Kayla," he mumbles. I move to walk away. "Better lose the loot. The noise of those brass rings will give you away before you even get where you're going. *If* you get where you're going." He stares at the ceiling. "Not many people know how the hallways move like I do."

I take two of the brass rings out of my pockets. Jax motions for me to take out more. Ugh. I remove the third and leave the fourth safely in my skirt. One can't do any harm. I drop the three of them in a bin of arrows near the door. Someone is going to be really happy when they score those beauties. "Fine," I say begrudgingly. "If you really want to know, I'm following Flora, okay? She seems sketchy if you ask me. First she's in the woods, and now I've caught her going down a hallway instead of evacuating."

"Being headmistress means she has to make sure all her students are out before she leaves," Jax says. "You realize that, right?"

"Yes, but it still seems fishy," I say. "I want to see what she's up to for myself. If you have a problem with that, you can just go. But don't tell anyone you saw me." I point a finger at him. "You still owe me for the other day."

Jax looks down the hallway. "Fine. I'll stick with you." He motions for me to walk. "After you, my lady."

I don't like his mocking tone, but I let it slide and head down one of the two hallways still open. We cross to another classroom (Wand training! Who knew?), head out a secret panel in the back, and then walk down another empty hallway. Halfway through, the hallway in front of us disappears.

Instead of being annoyed, Jax breaks into a small smile. "Even better," I hear him say as he pulls me down the new hallway and through a small door behind a staircase leading to the boys' dormitories. The new passageway we're in clearly doesn't see much foot traffic. Cobwebs brush past my face as we move swiftly downward where the air is much cooler. It's creepy in here. I don't like this.

"You want to spy on Flora? Then I know the best way to see her office without actually being seen," Jax says. "We're going to come up right underneath it."

"How'd you find this route?" I ask as Jax covers the only mirror in the hallway so far with his jacket to block Miri.

"Our teachers are former villains," Jax says. "Don't think you're the first person who wanted to check out Flora. I've done it too and have never found a thing."

"There's always a first time," I say, unconvinced. Down, down, down we descend to where the walls are mossy and there is a faint odor that my nose is not loving. When we reach the end of a hallway, I see a grate. Jax removes it and hands it to me.

"Come on," he whispers, and his voice echoes in the narrow duct. "We're just a few feet away from her office, so be *quiet*."

I'm fairly petite, but I hear the narrow passageway creak as I shimmy. It's hot, and I'm starting to feel claustrophobic. I've done a lot of things to pull off a job before. Crawling through an air vent is not one of them. I'm about to whisper just that when Jax stops near a large shaft of light above his head. He puts his finger to his lips and motions me over. I look up and see a familiar desk and standing lamp. We're underneath Flora's office.

"I don't see anyone up there," Jax says. "Happy?"

I peer through the grate, trying to get a closer look. The room does look empty. Darn. "I guess." I turn away quickly, and the lone brass ring in my pocket bounces out and hits the bottom of the air vent. Jax and I look at each other. He starts to laugh.

"You kept a drape clip?" He holds his stomach.

"It's brass!" I say, and that's when I hear a high-pitched squawk. "What was that?"

"Harlow's pesty crow?" Jax suggests, but his face says he's not convinced. He looks through the bars again. "Kind of loud for Aldo though, isn't it?"

A shadow flies across the grate so quickly that we barely

have a second to react. I hear a loud thud and see claws stretching through the bars. Jax quickly removes his hands.

SCREECH!

The sound is so loud my ears are ringing. That is definitely not Aldo.

The screeching only gets louder, and then the grate above us starts to move. Jax begins to pull me back just as a hairy claw pulls the grate clear off and a face peers down inside.

"What the—?" Jax starts to say as two glowing red eyes stare back at us.

The shape of the eyes, the claws…it's so familiar. "Gargoyles," I say almost to myself, and then I hear the ear-piercing sound again.

"Gargoyles aren't real," Jax tells me.

That's the last thing I hear him say before one flies through the grate after us.

CHAPTER 10

We've Got Company

Jax pushes me forward. "*Run!*"

I don't have to be told twice. With one hand I scoop up the brass ring, and with the other I pull my body forward through the grate, moving as fast as my hands and knees will take me. I hear more thuds echoing through the duct. More than one of those beasts is after us.

Gargoyles are real. Gargoyles are real. I knew *I saw one move!*

Their high-pitched wails are so loud that Jax and I are actually forced to stop for a second to cover our ears. Out of the corner of my eye, I see them. They're wrinkly and dark gray with red eyes and long wings that fold under themselves, but the long, sharp claws on their hands and feet frighten me the most. One lets out a long wail when he sees us and Jax shoves me forward again, shaking me from my trance.

My heart is pounding, and I can hear their nails tapping at the grate as I fly forward, seeing a light at the end of the tunnel. I throw myself out of it. I am relieved to see Jax right behind me. I run for the grate, prepared to put it back in place the minute Jax is clear to hold off the gargoyles. It seems like a good plan until I see Jax's face twist in pain, and he begins sliding backward into the tunnel.

"Gilly!" he yells.

I drop the grate and grab Jax's hands, pulling as hard as I can and get nowhere. It's like we're locked in a tug-of-war and Jax is the rope. The screeching makes it almost impossible to hear, but I see Jax's lips moving.

"My shirt pocket!" he yells, and I let go of one of his hands to reach inside his shirt. I pull out a vintage pocket watch that looks like it cost a fortune. *What's this got to do with anything?* I think as another wail from the gargoyles makes me wince. "Open it, and aim it at them. *Them!* Not me!" he yells.

I open the watch and hear Jax yell a word I don't understand. Then I am momentarily blinded as a bolt shoots from the watch and hits the gargoyles. Their screams are deafening, but their hold on Jax relaxes. I yank Jax so hard that the two of us go crashing to the floor.

"Give me that," Jax says, pulling the watch from my hand. "I think you singed my pants!" Sure enough, his pants are smoking. The hems are shredded where the gargoyles grabbed him. Tiny drops of blood drip down his calves.

"You could say thank you!" I bark as I try to stand up, but my legs are quivering.

"For almost getting us killed?" Jax yells back. "You just *had* to spy on Flora."

Then a wail stops us both in our tracks. We look at each other, and I know we're both thinking the same thing. Those gargoyles are not dead.

"Shoot the watch thing again!" I say, scrambling to my feet and grabbing his arm to run.

"I can't! It only works once an hour." Jax takes the lead, pulling me along.

The shrieking intensifies as the gargoyles fly out of the duct and after us down the hall, picking up speed. "*Duck!*" I yell as one dives at Jax's head. The exit is just ahead of us. Just a few more feet. A few more… "*No!*" I scream as my shirt takes flight—and me along with it.

“Kick!” Jax yells, pulling on my leg. “Kick harder!”

The gargoyle’s face is so close I can smell its rancid breath. Its claws rip through my shirt and sink into my back. I scream and immediately my mind takes me to my siblings. I’m not going out like this. They need me. I kick harder, wiggling like a worm until my leg hits the gargoyle hard in the stomach.

The gargoyle wails and drops me. Jax breaks my fall, half catching me, half stumbling to the door, which he throws us both through. We slam it shut and lean against it as the gargoyles screech madly.

“I can’t hold it,” Jax yells, gritting his teeth as he pushes against the door.

“Me either,” I say, breathing heavily. My back is burning from the gargoyle’s scratches. “What are we going to do?”

I hear sparks and look up. An enraged Flora is holding a mirror with a stunning mermaid inside. “Move!” she commands us.

We don’t have to be told twice. A long bolt of light flies out of the mirror and zaps the door we were just holding shut. The door behind us flashes purple, and then the shrieking and pushing stops. The hall is eerily quiet.

“You two are lucky you knocked the jacket off the mirror

in the hallway." Flora sounds out of breath. "Or you would have been gargoyle food! What were you thinking—sneaking off instead of going to your evacuation stations?" she thunders.

"I thought I knew a shortcut," Jax says quickly. "Then we ran into those living statues." Jax gives me a look. I kind of think it says, "Now you owe me."

"How were we supposed to know the gargoyle statues were real creatures?" I ask Flora.

"No one knew they were real until half an hour ago!" Flora says, sounding exasperated. "That's why we had the evacuation—so the staff could stop them and students could get to safety, not use the time to sneak around the school!" Headmistress Flora purses her lips. "I'm disappointed in you, Miss Gillian. I thought you wanted your time here to go as smoothly as possible." Her face gets a little too close for comfort, and I smell roses, which always remind me of a funeral. "Go looking for trouble inside these walls, and trouble will find you. Now, both of you thank Madame Cleo for saving your lives."

"Thank you," we mumble.

"My pleasure, darlings," Cleo sings. "Pretty but foolish little darlings that you are. Who planted those things here, Flora?"

"I don't know, but I want every last statue removed until we figure that out." Flora smiles thinly. "As for you two, there is to be no talk of gargoyle statues coming alive and trying to rip students to shreds. I'd have to schedule extra therapy classes to deal with the reaction." She holds her head. "You'll both spend the next two *weeks* with Madame Cleo in detention for almost getting yourselves killed." Her eyes narrow. "And if you ever sneak off during a drill like that again, next time I'll make it four weeks—if you live to tell the tale."

"Yes, Headmistress Flora," Jax and I say dejectedly.

I thought gargoyles were tough. Detention with a sea siren might be worse.

Happily Ever After Scrolls

Brought to you by FairyWeb—magically appearing on scrolls throughout Enchantasia for the past ten years!

From the Sea's Biggest Menace to One of FTRS's Most Beloved Teachers: Say Hello to Madame Cleo!

by Beatrice Beez

Name: Madame Cleo (the mermaid formerly known as the "Sea Witch" or "Sea Siren," depending on who lived to tell the tale. No pun intended.)

Former Occupation: Scaring sailors, making fishy deals for personal gain, trying to destroy the Little Mermaid's chance at love

Current Occupation: After a memory-loss spell meant for a shark accidentally zapped Cleo instead, the Sea Siren's quest for villainy disappeared. She now teaches dance and etiquette to students at FTRS. "I couldn't be happier! Dance is… What were we talking about?"

Hobbies: Water aerobics, listening to classical music, attending Under the Sea balls

Strengths: Sorcery ("I may not know what I ate for lunch, but I could never forget a good spell!") and teaching good manners ("I love it when students say, 'Good morn, Madame Cleo.'")

Weakness: A lack of legs. "Breathing on land seems overrated. I see no need for a pair."

Likes: Shiny gifts and Rapunzel's shampoo ("The salt water does a number on my hair, darling.")

Hates: Sushi and high-pitched sounds

Love Life: "Who has time for men when you're trying to save Enchantasia from poor posture?"

Check back next week for more Fairy Tale Reform School Fifth Anniversary coverage.

CHAPTER 11

Something's Fishy

Headmistress Flora feels the need to hand-deliver me to Madame Cleo's detention the next day after classes, and I soon find myself standing in front of an oversized metal double door. I read the large plaque near the entrance: Warning! If doors are locked, do not magically open. Tank may be refilling or flooding!

"Where are we? The aquarium?" I joke.

"You *could* call it that," Flora says, "but I wouldn't. This is the entrance to Madame Cleo's home, and she's gracious enough to invite you in for detention."

I look down at my plaid jumper and navy vest. "I'm not dressed for a swim."

"A swimsuit won't be necessary," the Wicked Stepmother

says cryptically. "You'll start etiquette classes here later this week as well. You'll see we keep students busy. It keeps you from getting bored and, shall we say, interested in less savory extracurricular activities." She gives me a long, hard glance.

She means things like thieving, brawling with gargoyles, and spying on villains.

Flora turns on her heels and walks away. "Enjoy your afternoon, Miss Gillian."

I pull on the double doors to see if they're locked due to a water leak. Unfortunately, they open. When I slip inside, I feel the temperature drop significantly, along with the lighting. The spacious but dimly lit room has a two-story ceiling but no windows. *Slurp!* I hear the doors lock and seal behind me, and I wonder if I've been led into some sort of trap.

I look for another exit, and that's when I see a giant fish tank shimmering in the darkness. Fish of every size and color swim by, dodging between bright coral and sea plants, and hiding among the giant rocks nestled inside. I put my face near the glass and peer into the tank, which seems to go back for miles. Aren't we inside a castle?

The torches flicker, and then the doors open. Several students run—or fly—inside. It's mass chaos to get in before the final bell. When it tolls, the doors shut behind us, and with another *slurp*, I hear them seal shut again.

"Hey, sticky fingers." Jax smiles. "How are you feeling?" He's changed out of his uniform and is wearing an FTRS T-shirt and gym shorts that show his bandaged legs.

"Okay," I say. I have no dirt on Flora that could spring me early, and I can't tell anyone that the gargoyle statues around school came alive and attacked Jax and me. I am just super. "Yesterday was…weird, huh?"

Jax's face is filled with shadows in the low light. "That's one way to put it."

"What do you think those things wanted?" I whisper. "Where'd they come from?"

"I don't know and I don't care," Jax says, twirling his book bag's strap in his hands. "Look, we almost became gargoyle stew yesterday. You need to think like a thief. Stop worrying about what Flora's doing, and worry more about yourself."

Think like a thief. I always have…and now I'm stuck here unable to help my siblings. Is anyone making sure Hamish doesn't eat glue and Felix doesn't stay up all night by candlelight to read? Are they getting enough to eat?

A light in the aquarium grinds our conversation to a halt.

I turn toward the tank and watch as a blur shoots toward the glass. Once the water stops moving, I see Madame Cleo, who until yesterday I'd only seen in that mirror frying up gargoyles. She is the most beautiful mermaid I've ever seen. Her purple hair is decorated with sea flowers and shells that match her shell top. Her skin and long, dark-green fishtail shimmer brightly.

"Hello, darlings!" Madame Cleo's voice echoes through the room. How does she do that? Other mermaids have to hold up cue cards in class to talk. I guess being the ultimate sea siren makes for powerful magic.

"Good afternoon, Madame Cleo," we say in unison and either bow or curtsy.

Since I have little use for curtsies, mine is rusty. I bang into the girl next to me.

"Watch your step, clumsy." The girl turns toward me, and I stare into the eyes of someone who is definitely half cat. Or maybe werewolf? Who can tell?

"She didn't mean it, Gayle." Jax wastes no time in moving us to a less hostile place on the floor.

Madame Cleo's voice is like a song. "I'm disappointed you're in detention, but if you're here, you might as well learn something that will enhance your lives." She claps her hands, and a sparkly disco ball descends from the ceiling as music begins to play. "Today we will be concentrating on the dance of love. The Fire Step."

The Fire Step is a complicated dance that is usually done at weddings. When Mother and Father thought they were getting an invite to Ella's wedding (they didn't, FYI), they practiced for a month and still couldn't figure it out. I've never attempted it.

"First, let me take attendance for our headmistress." Madame Cleo swims around the tank, playing with her pearl necklace. She looks right at Jax. "Jackson! Lovely to see you again."

I snort. "Jackson?"

Jax's face colors. "Not a word," he says through gritted teeth.

"And Gillian." Cleo smiles. "We meet again. Now where is Jocelyn?" Cleo asks and immediately people start to squirm. Helmut tries to squish himself behind a rock jutting out of the wall. "Jocey?" Madame's voice goes up an octave. "Don't be shy. You can't get more detention *in* detention."

There is a poof of purple smoke, and Jocelyn materializes in the middle of the room. Dressed all in black from head to toe, she looks a lot like Harlow. "Good afternoon, Madame Cleo!" Jocelyn does a perfect curtsy. "Sorry I'm late. I was with my sister."

Madame Cleo laughs, and her hair slowly turns from purple to turquoise. "I know when Harlow starts talking, it's hard to get her to stop! Thank you both for the lovely coral arrangement for my birthday."

"Of course!" Jocelyn says. "Harlow and I would never miss your special day. And I would never skip detention, especially when there are so many interesting people in here having such fascinating conversations." She looks directly at me and Jax and grins.

Did she hear us talking about the gargoyles? How?

"It's a pity you're even here, Jocey, but since so many students saw you cast that spell on Maxine yesterday afternoon, I had no choice."

I'd heard the news from Kayla this morning. At her evacuation station, Jocelyn got bored and cast a spell on Maxine that made her right ear as big as her head. She was in the infirmary recovering. I visited Maxine at lunch to check on her. "It's okay," she'd said when I asked what happened. "I'm used to Jocelyn picking on me."

Well, I still don't like it—and I don't like Jocelyn either.

"It's not true. I have no idea how that happened to Maxine." Jocelyn shakes her head. "But like my sis, I take my lumps with dignity."

"A proper lady!" Madame Cleo marvels. "Well then, shall we… Oh hi, class! When did you all get here?"

"Memory-loss spell," Jax whispers. "Sometimes she forgets what she's doing. Last week, detention was only thirty minutes because she forgot what time we came in."

"You were teaching the Fire Step, Madame Cleo," Helmut says. Within seconds, his head snaps back. "Ouch! Who hit me?" I see Jocelyn smirk.

"The Fire Step! Yes, that's right!" she says. The sound of a fast instrumental song floats through the room. Madame Cleo closes her eyes and sways back and forth. The fish around her do the same. "Done properly, the Fire Step can make all the difference between catching a prince and a prince's footman. You don't have many afternoons to master this dance. Royal Day is just days away."

"Lucky us," I mumble.

Jax looks amused. "What did the royals do to you? Steal your glass slipper?"

"Kind of." Jax looks intrigued. "My dad's a shoemaker, and the orders for the glass slippers he was making were handed over to Ella's fairy godmother so she could conjure them up herself. That's made a real dent in a family business that was barely making ends meet to begin with." I sigh. "And yet my sister still idolizes those girls."

"They took my father's farm to build a summer castle for themselves," Jax says. "I haven't liked the royals since."

"Typical." I shake my head.

Cleo claps her hands and the sound echoes through the room. "Partner up!"

Jax holds out his hand. "Shall we?"

"I'm not a Fire Step kind of girl." I stumble over my words. I've never danced with someone who isn't my brother. And having your brothers dance on your feet doesn't count.

"Gillian, darling," Madame Cleo sings, but there is a hard tone to her voice. "Everyone must participate."

My cheeks flush slightly. "Fine, but don't step on my toes," I tell Jax. "Do you even know how to—whoa." Jax takes my hands and whirls me around the room. The whirling part I could do blindfolded, but the rest is a mystery.

"Just watch what I do," he tells me as he double claps,

then does a crisscross motion with his feet and changes direction all in a matter of seconds. He's really good. When we get to the part in the dance where we switch partners, then switch back, Jax manages to take two, then return to me before I even do my first spin around.

"I didn't realize you had use for the Fire Step on the farm," I say over the music.

"There wasn't," Jax says. His violet eyes are practically purple in this light. "A lot of time in detention has made me an excellent dancer."

"So I see." I double clap, but on the wrong beat. *Oops.*

People glide around the room, switching directions. There's a lot of clapping and slapping one's heel and snapping of fingers at just the right moment, but I'm pretty sure I couldn't master this dance even with a year's worth of detention.

The only one partnerless is Jocelyn, not that she seems concerned. With a quick poof, a shadow appears in front of her, taking the outline of a boy. Madame Cleo looks over at Jocelyn curiously but doesn't say anything. I guess being the Evil Queen's sister means you can get away with a lot. Jocelyn takes the shadow's nonexistent hands and begins to dance around the room. She bangs into me on her way by, and I fall into Jax.

"Don't let her rattle you," Jax says.

Before I can say anything, we have to switch partners again and I'm with Helmut.

"You're the new girl, right?" says Helmut, who looks more terrified than impressed. "I got caught breaking into the Enchantasia Market one too many times. I have a thing for the baker's cinnamon rolls." He blushes. "What are you in for?"

"Kind of the same thing," I say, wincing as Helmut steps on both my feet. "Family's got to eat, you know. I took what I needed to survive."

"I thought cobblers just ate shoe leather," Jocelyn says as she and her shadow dance by us.

I've had enough of this one. "I never have, but if you want to try eating leather, I'm happy to shove some down your throat." Helmut gulps loudly.

Jocelyn smiles eerily. "Students who shoot their mouth off to me don't last long."

I stop dancing. "Are you threatening me?" Helmut slowly backs away. "I thought FTRS was all about reforming yourself."

Jocelyn smiles evilly. "It is, but who's to say what we're reforming ourselves into next? Stop snooping around this school, or believe me, thief, you'll regret it." I feel a chill go down my spine. "I have powers you can't even dream of."

"I'm not scared," I say as Jax tugs on my arm to steer me away.

Jocelyn's eyes narrow. "You will be when you see what I can do. Watch." Her lips begin to move, and a glow emits from her eyes. Jax shoves me out of the way, but he needn't bother. I'm not the one Jocelyn is toying with. Gayle lets out an ear-piercing scream, and her troll partner flies backward, hitting one of the torches on the wall, which falls and causes a small fire that short-circuits the music. Students see Jocelyn chanting and run for cover, but Helmut begins to wail and falls to the floor. Within seconds, most of my classmates are low to the ground, covering their ears. Her spell has affected everyone but Jax and me.

"Stop it!" I say, but Jocelyn ignores me. I turn to Jax. "We have to do something!" As I say the words, I can hear Jax's earlier advice in my head. *Just take care of yourself.* But I can't just stand here and watch others suffer because Jocelyn wants to teach me a lesson

"What is that sound?" Cleo cries, holding her ears. "Jocelyn, help me!"

The Sea Siren is seemingly blind to the fact Jocelyn is the one causing the noise. Kayla told me Cleo can't handle loud sounds, and it must be true. I watch as Cleo's hair flashes pink, then purple, then green before she begins to scream so loudly that bubbles take over the tank and the floor actually begins to quake. Soon Cleo's gentle demeanor is gone, and for a second I can see a flash of the sea siren she must have been. It's pretty terrifying. And that's before the tank begins to crack.

"She'll drown us all!" an ogre says, pushing his way to the exit.

Jax beats him to it, and I fear he's abandoning us. Instead, he pulls out his pocket watch and zaps the lock. Students stream out of the room, Helmut helping Gayle to the door. In terror, a pixie flies by me and bangs into a wall. Jax scoops her up. All the while, Jocelyn continues to chant, a smug smile on her face.

When I look back, Madame Cleo has passed out and is floating in the middle of the tank. Enough is enough. I jump on Jocelyn's back and try to knock her to the ground.

"Get off me!" Jocelyn yells, spinning around so fast that I should fly off, but I have a great grip. (Father's delivery horse, Lion's Mane, is as wild as they come.) Jocelyn twists and bucks, but I hang on. At least I've gotten her to stop chanting.

Suddenly we're hit from the side, and we fall to the floor. When I look up, Jax is holding the disco ball that was hanging from the ceiling.

"You're going to regret this, thief." Jocelyn holds her cheek, which is scratched and bleeding. "You too, farm boy. Those gargoyles are nothing compared to what you'll see next." Purple smoke rises around her, and then she's gone.

I'm still choking on the smoke when Jax gives me a hand and helps me up. "Now you owe me two favors."

"I thought you didn't like helping people," I say in between coughs.

Jax shrugs. "I figured keeping the whole class from drowning was more for my benefit than theirs. Fewer students in class mean more focus on me." I shake my head.

Madame Cleo moans, and we turn back to the tank. She's starting to come to. I bang on it, knowing that's the opposite of what you're supposed to do to a fish tank, but I don't know what else to do. "Madame Cleo? Are you okay?"

Cleo's green eyes snap open like she's in a trance. "*Once a villain, always a villain,*" she says in a monotone voice that sounds nothing like her own. "*Evil is coming, and it can't be stopped. Enchantasia, beware…*" Her mouth curves into a sinister smile. "*Fairy Tale Reform School will burn.*"

The hair on my arms stands up.

"She's under some sort of spell." Jax bangs harder on the glass. "Madame Cleo?"

Cleo's eyes flutter wildly, and then her body relaxes. "Darlings!" She smiles. "How good of you to come to detention. Is it just you two today?"

Jax and I look at each other. Did that really just happen?

"Uh, yeah," Jax says.

"Great!" Madame Cleo smiles and pets a sea horse that swims by her. The thing is still trembling with fear from her recent outburst. "Then let's dance, shall we?"

Chapter 12

Royal Day

"Good morning, Fairy Tale Reform School!" Headmistress Flora's unusually cheery voice booms through the great hall. "Today is the day we've been waiting for. After five years, the princesses will be arriving any minute to visit our fine school!"

Cheers ripple through the packed student crowd (attendance was mandatory) like we're at an über-popular Troll-tally Fantastic concert.

Flora has rolled out the red carpet—literally—for our royal guests. A gold "Welcome to Fairy Tale Reform School!" banner hangs over the great hall's archway, and the FTRS band is practicing the royal processional while *Happily Ever After Scrolls* reporters stand anxiously near the school's two-story front doors with quills and paper at the ready. We're all standing at attention. Tanks have been set up along the back wall of the hall for the mer-students, and Madame Cleo has been beamed in on one of Miri's mirrors. There's even a fairyographer ready to capture the princesses' arrival.

"I expect you to put your *best* foot—or fin—forward today," Flora says. Professor Harlow and Professor Wolfington flank the headmistress, each in long, green embroidered robes, while Jocelyn—shocker—stands nearby. "We have a list of activities the royals will be attending, which you should have received this morning along with starched uniforms."

My favorite work boots seem to have gone missing. The only shoes I could find this morning were the ugly, black standard ones we all wear.

Clever, Flora. Very clever.

"These uniforms itch," grumbles Jax, who is standing next to me. His hair is slicked back, and the buttons on his shirt gleam even brighter than his shoes.

"They make us look good," says Ollie as he makes his way through the crowd to reach us. I watch as he produces a crystal bottle from inside his shirt sleeve. A few feet away

I hear someone say, "Hey! What happened to my cologne?" Ollie doesn't blink an eye as he dabs away. The musky smell makes my eyes water. "You never know when one of these princesses is going to ditch her prince and go looking for a more worldly fella."

"Today is a very important day for our school," Flora adds. "We want the princesses to recognize FTRS's positive impact on the kingdom of Enchantasia."

Kayla snorts. "She means she's desperate for them to throw us a royal ball. *Ick!* The idea of curtsying to royals makes me want to cough up my breakfast."

I didn't realize Kayla was a royal hater like me. Makes me realize how little the two of us have really talked since I got here almost two weeks ago.

A group of girls wearing hot pink Royal Ladies-in-Waiting sashes pushes past us. *Groan.* I saw these girls in our dorm common room last night, and they couldn't stop bragging about how they were the royal school escorts for the day. As if I'd ever want that job.

"Someone got up on the wrong side of the bed," I joke. "You shouldn't have gotten up so early to help prepare the royal feast, Kayla."

Jax gives her a look. "You did? Why'd you volunteer if you hate the royals so much?"

"Extra-credit, and I'm not tired. I'm fine," Kayla snaps. "Can we just stop talking about this?"

She doesn't look fine. Kayla's eyes have black rings under them, and her short, blond hair is unusually unkempt. She didn't even put on her pressed uniform. Well, if she wanted to talk about whatever is bothering her, I assume she would. I think that's what roommates do—not that we've done that, other than the night when she told me about her family.

I notice Flora touching the marble statue of a king in the foyer and smiling up at it. I like that one much better than the gargoyles that have disappeared from the halls. If students noticed, they haven't said anything. "Who is that statue of?" I ask the group.

"King Jerrod," Ollie tells me. "Enchantasia's first royal. Rumor has it he went from a thief to king overnight. We think he's somewhat of an idol for Flora. She kept that statue in her private home until this week."

"Headmistress Flora," Mira announces breathlessly. "The princesses have just passed through the school gates."

"Places, everyone!" Flora says, and the school orchestra begins to play.

"This is so ridiculous," Kayla says. She's obviously one of the few who feel that way, because within moments there is a collective gasp from the entire hall as the doors open, and we see the princesses standing there in the flesh.

"Presenting Enchantasia's royal court," Miri announces in a regal voice I've never heard her use before. "Princess Ella, Princess Rose, Princess Snow, and Princess Rapunzel."

There's no denying that each one is prettier than the last. The dewy skin, the glossy hair—perfect little packages of beauty. But instead of being envious (like the fairy next to me silently shooting death rays at them) or emotional (like Maxine, who is holding a hand-painted sign that says "Snow, You Melt My Heart") or lovesick (like Ollie, who is holding a Rapunzel poster), all I can think about is how much work must go into being one of them. And all that arm-waving and smiling. It must be exhausting.

But my classmates drink it up. They're chanting, screaming, applauding, and practically throwing themselves at the princesses as they walk down the carpet laid out in their honor. Usually the only time we get a glimpse of royalty is when they're riding by in a carriage waving a white-gloved hand to the adoring masses. Today I can see Cinderella's royal blue gown up close. Her beaded skirt is so poufy you could hide half my bedroom furniture under it.

I watch as Ella reaches her former stepmonster. For a moment, the excitement seems to die down as we all wonder how the two will handle their first face-to-face encounter since the big shoe dilemma. Headmistress Flora demurely curtsies. Then Ella curtsies back.

"Whoa." Jax whistles. "I didn't see that one coming."

"Maybe they've put all the bad blood behind them," Maxine suggests, hovering near the edge of our group. "Maybe Ella has forgiven Flora. I mean, she did agree to come today, right?"

Kayla makes a face. "Who cares what the real reason is? We should be focusing on Ella's gown. She could have fed my whole village with what it cost to make that dress." She sighs. "I've had enough. I'd rather go to stargazing class than listen to all this fawning." She gives me a look as a boy next to us faints at the sight of Rapunzel. "And you know how much I hate stargazing."

"Do you want me to walk you down there?" Kayla's acting so weird, and I can't tell if it's me or her. Ever since I heard

Madame Cleo make that spooky prediction in detention, I've been on edge. Jax says I'm worrying for nothing. ("The Sea Siren doesn't remember her name half the time. You think she's going to be right about a villain uprising?")

"No, I'm fine. You have scroll works in the totally opposite direction." Kayla manages a smile. "I'll see you afterward in gym."

"Wait up. I'm walking your way." Jax links arms with Kayla. "Ollie and I may even sneak into stargazing to avoid wand work."

"I'm thinking of doing a sleight-of-hand trick to conjure up a hall pass," Ollie tells me gleefully.

I wish I could do that trick. The last place I want to go later today is gym to kiss up to the royals. When it's time, I practically have to drag myself to the gym locker room to get changed. On my way there, I get stuck behind a bunch of gossiping Royal Ladies-in-Waiting.

"I heard the glass cracked in the middle of Madame Cleo's ballroom-dancing presentation!" the Royal Ladies' captain is saying. "It practically flooded the room. They said Snow got completely soaked."

I immediately think of Madame Cleo's prediction again.

Maxine pushes ahead of me and grips the most popular Royal Lady-in-Waiting's arm. "Were the princesses all right?"

"Headmistress Flora took Snow to her chambers to find her something suitable to wear 'til a servant from the castle arrives with dry clothes," says a royal wannabe. "I'm just upset we didn't think to bring them extra gowns ourselves!"

Another member shakes the first one. "Hold it together." The other girl nods and takes big, gulping breaths. "We can make up lost ground during the luncheon sing-along."

"How could Madame Cleo's tank break?" I ask more importantly, and the girls turn to look at me with disdain. Obviously not being a Royal Lady-in-Waiting means I'm not allowed to comment. "I thought it was made of the strongest glass there is."

"Nothing's strong enough to compete with black magic," says Jocelyn, walking past us. The torches lighting the hallway dim as if they sense her darkness. "The crack in the tank, the swarm of pernicious peony ants that were accidentally released in the botany lab, the poisoned fruit found in the cafeteria at the breakfast buffet." She looks at me directly. "No one should cross the dark side."

"Poisoned fruit?" Maxine's lazy eye does a one-eighty.

Jocelyn takes a bite of an apple. "Helmut's at the infirmary with Princess Rapunzel, who got a nasty peony-ant bite on her nose."

One of the Royal Ladies pulls off her pink sash, and it hits Maxine in the face. "I'm told Ella gave Flora her permission this morning for us to hold an anniversary ball at FTRS next week. Now that's never going to happen! What are we going to do, ladies?"

Who cares about the royal ball? I want to know whether Flora would host Royal Day if she is up to no good.

Maybe.

Azalea is waiting as we approach the gym locker room. She student teaches in our class, and she doesn't look thrilled. "You're keeping Harlow waiting, and you all know how much Harlow likes to be kept waiting."

"Harlow?" I ask. "Where's Madame Tilly?" Tilly is our ogre-rific gym coach. With the warts on her nose, her unibrow, and the bad overbite, she's kind of tough to look at, but she's the nicest teacher in this joint.

"Harlow is taking over your class to prevent any more incidents." Azalea adjusts the bodice of her pale-peach gown. I look around. There's no sign of Kayla. "One more misstep and the princesses are out of here, so suit up. Harlow wants you to impress them with your fencing skills."

"Excellent." Jocelyn gives me a smug smile.

"*Happily Ever After Scrolls* is here too," Azalea adds. "Let's make a good impression, ladies. It would be nice if one story from today could be about how our reform school is actually reforming students rather than injuring them."

"Somehow I don't see how using swords will help," I point out.

Azalea's pretty green eyes narrow at me. "No one asked for your opinion, Gilly." She opens the door to the locker room, and I look at Maxine. She shrugs and heads to her cubby to get out armor.

Like every other room at FTRS, our gym has gotten a makeover for Royal Day. Silk banners hang from each wall touting our various sports teams (Magic Carpet Racing! Castle Storming! Synchronized Snake Charming!). A banquet table sits along the back wall, covered with a silk tablecloth and bouquets of lilies. Professor Harlow has changed out of her gown and is wearing fitted fencing gear with a tiara replacing her helmet.

I see Jax, Ollie, and the other boys in our class emerge from the boys' dressing room, and I make a beeline for them. I yank Jax away from Ollie without explanation.

"Have you heard what's been happening all morning?" I say, sounding shrill. "It's got to have something to do with Madame Cleo's prediction!"

"Don't get your knickers in a knot," Jax says. "It's probably just a coincidence."

Is Jax daft? "Something is definitely going on! Flora has to be behind it, or Jocelyn—she knew about the gargoyles. What if Flora is planning to burn down her own school?"

I look around the room worriedly. Jocelyn and Harlow are talking quietly in a corner, and Headmistress Flora is chatting with Princess Snow. I glance at the Royal Ladies-in-Waiting. They're handing the princesses baskets of flowers. Sleeping Beauty is watching us, but Ella is stifling a yawn, and Rapunzel is holding an ice bag to her nose, which is a nasty shade of blue. Okay, nothing unusual at the moment, but something *has* to be up. I need dirt on someone—and quick. I've got to get out of this place and back to my brothers and sisters while I'm still in one piece to do it!

"This is why I told you to only worry about yourself." Jax runs a hand through his hair. "I should have bailed when I had the chance myself." I glare at him. He's not helping. "At least Flora called in the Dwarf Police Squad for the rest of the day."

I look at Pete and Olaf and resist the urge to blurt out, "I didn't do it."

"Fencers, please get in position," Azalea interrupts, handing us each a sword.

The cold handle of the silver sword gives me an instant feeling of calm. No wonder the Evil Queen fences. I wish she didn't coach the team because I would actually try out to be on it. I bet I'd win my matches too. That's what I always want: to win. I still don't know what the future holds for me, but I know I'm not meant to be a cobbler. I want a job that I'm in control of. Not one that is handed to me by the royals.

Jocelyn walks by me, swinging her sword at her side, and I slide out of the way before she can "accidentally" pierce my gym shorts. The two of us glare at each other as we walk into the center of the room. I hear the gym doors swing open and Kayla runs inside. She's wearing her gym uniform, but her hair is noticeably wet and there is a pink stain on her arm. Her skin is whiter than usual, and her wings are not fluttering. She takes a sword from a less-than-pleased Azalea and races over to Jax and me.

"Are you okay?" I ask.

Kayla wipes sweat from her brow. "The hallways weren't working right, and I couldn't find my way to the gym. It's no big deal." She sounds testy again, so I let it drop.

Harlow adjusts the tiara on her head as she walks our way. "Sorry to interrupt your tea party, ladies, but I'm speaking," she whispers. "Students, please turn to the person to your left and prepare for an assault." I look at her blankly. "Jocelyn," Harlow says, sounding bored.

Jocelyn sighs. "That's fencing speak for a friendly battle, Cobbler."

"Sweet! I love friendly battles!" Ollie turns to Jax at the same time I do. "Aw, dude. Tell me I turned right instead of left?"

"You turned right instead of left," we say, and he turns the other way.

Jax grins like he's won our duel before he's even lifted a sword.

"Nice try, but you're going down." I rest my hand on my sword.

"You don't even know how to use that thing," Jax says.

"And you do?" I joke. He probably does. He's been here longer than me.

"We're going to start with a balestra followed by a lunge and then—" Harlow is cut off by the sound of a crash from above that sends glass raining down on the room. Jax and I put our hands over our heads and duck for cover, and that's when I hear the screeching.

Gargoyles. My stomach lurches as my classmates begin to scream and run in different directions. A few are pulled into the air by the beasties, and I hear the red-alert siren sound just like it did that day in Wolfington's class.

This time it's definitely not a drill.

I immediately start to cough as a thick, purple fog fills the room.

We're done for.

Chapter 13

Sword Play

I'll never see my siblings again.

I'll never get to say I'm sorry to Anna for stealing that clip on her birthday.

I'll never get to make Mother and Father proud of me.

The last thought startles me. I didn't even know I cared what Father thought of me. I need to find a way to still make that happen. I can't worry about what's going on with Flora or Madame Cleo's prediction. I have to get out of here and get home.

I take a deep breath and cover my nose with my shirt in case the gas is poisonous. Then I feel someone grab my hand and see Jax through the haze. He shoves me into a corner as Ollie crawls over to us, along with Maxine and some Royal

Ladies-in-Waiting who are crying. I can't see Jocelyn anywhere in this fog. All I hear is screeching and screaming.

An exit. I need to find an exit. And Kayla. I look around frantically for my roommate and see her stumbling toward us. I reach out and yank her into our little cluster. "Are you okay?"

Kayla covers her face with her hands and starts to mumble strangely. "I didn't do it. I swear! I am nothing. She's right. I'm nothing. I'm sorry. So sorry." She dissolves into tears and rocks back and forth on the floor. Maxine puts an arm around her, and Jax and I look at each other worriedly. Once this fog fades, the gargoyles will have us.

"Dude, what the heck is happening? Wait, is that…is that a gargoyle?" Ollie manages to get out in between hacking fits. We all dive to the floor when we see wings appear out of the fog above. A gargoyle grabs hold of one of the Ladies-in-Waiting and takes off again. She screams and kicks, but it's no use. She's a goner. "I thought gargoyles were statues," Ollie says, his eyes widening. "Those nasty beasties are real?"

I hear a loud *slurp* and assume someone has just magically sealed the gym doors like they do in Madame Cleo's detention room. I can hear Pete shouting orders to Olaf, and then in the next moment, the room is quiet. As the fog begins to lift, I can see that the gargoyles have rounded up the princesses and placed them in a corner of the room in some sort of glowing bubble, along with a few unlucky students. The dwarf squad is tied up in its own bubble nearby. A lot of help they were. One of the gargoyles drops Azalea onto the royals' bubble, and I watch as it sucks her in and drops her to the floor.

Okay, if I hang on to my sword, maybe I can fight my way to a gym door and pick a lock. I'm not waiting around any longer. I start to get up and prepare to run.

"What are you doing?" Jax hisses. "Stay down!"

A screech nearby distracts me, and I look up in time to see Jocelyn get picked up. Maxine gives out a little gasp, and her one eyeball starts to bounce up and down like a ball. Jocelyn doesn't go far. I watch as she swings wildly with her sword and nicks one of the gargoyle's legs.

"Yes!" Maxine cheers.

The gargoyle drops Jocelyn like a hot potato. She falls to the ground and bumps her head as the fog evaporates. We stare at her as she lies there motionless.

That's when I notice that Flora and Harlow are the only teachers not inside a bubble. Just as I'm about to yell "villain," I notice they're both as still as statues, like they're in some sort of trance. I need to make a break for it. On the count of one, two…

"Why isn't Harlow helping her sister?" one of the Ladies-in-Waiting wails.

"I don't know and I don't care," Jax says. "All I know is it's time we—"

Before Jax can finish his sentence, I see wings descend from the sky and our group scatters as Jax is picked up. Like Jocelyn, he grabs for his sword, but his falls out of his holster along with his trusty pocket watch.

"Jax!" I yell, and Kayla whimpers.

She's practically catatonic. "What did I do?" she says to herself over and over as Maxine rubs her back worriedly.

Jax struggles to break free, but he can't. All I can do is watch as he's sucked into the same bubble as the princesses. Out of the corner of my eye, I notice Harlow walking toward the immobilized princesses and Jax as if in a trance.

Now's my chance to move. I'm sure I can make it to the door before Harlow turns around, but Jax… How can I leave him behind when he's helped me so many times? I look over at the bubble, and the two of us make eye contact. I can almost hear his thoughts. *You owe me.*

Grr...I know. But what can I do?

Then I see Harlow raise her sword. The Ladies-in-Waiting around me gasp.

"We've got to help Jax," Ollie says hurriedly, and I watch him feel around in his pockets for some of his magic tricks. "Maybe if I could drop a smoke bomb..."

"This room is smoky enough," I say as Maxine and Kayla start to cry. A Royal Lady-in-Waiting hands them her handkerchief to share. "Give me a minute to think."

"Harlow! Stop!" Flora warns, her voice sharp.

For some strange reason, Flora can't move. Are she and Harlow under some sort of spell? If Harlow hears her, she doesn't listen.

"No," I hear Harlow say, and she throws her sword through the air. Maxine screams as the sword hits the bubble and bounces off it. The gargoyles jump up and down excitedly as Harlow picks up a few of the discarded swords on the ground and aims another one at the bubble. This time, the sword pierces the top, and I hear everyone inside scream. I can see Jax urging the princesses to squeeze as far back in the bubble as they can go. She aims again. This sword pierces the bubble and hits Princess Snow in the arm. She crumbles to the ground, and some of the girls around me burst into tears.

"She's going after Snow," Maxine says. "She has to be. She's going to keep aiming 'til she gets Snow—and anyone in the way."

Harlow throws another sword, and it pierces the bottom of the bubble, hitting a student in the shoe. He hops up and down in pain. The gargoyles screech happily. Jax gives me a desperate look.

"I need to distract the gargoyles," I say. "Anyone have a clue how to deal with the nasties?"

Kayla is shaking so violently I fear she's going to be ill. Then she pulls a bag out of her pocket with something purple inside. "Give them radishes. They'll put the gargoyles right to sleep."

I don't ask how she knows that. There's no time.

Ollie grabs the bag and begins passing out radishes. Maxine starts to toss them. I'm amazed as a gargoyle picks one up and pops it in his mouth. In a moment, he's sleeping like a baby. Soon the other students around me are doing the same, and gargoyles start dropping like flies. But that does nothing to stop Harlow.

"I must do what the huntsman should have done years ago," Harlow says in a monotone voice. "Send a dagger straight through her heart." Harlow makes a jerky movement in Snow's direction.

"Harlow, please! Fight this!" Flora begs as Harlow uses magic to pick up a handful of swords and aim them all at the bubble at the same time. I watch as Jax jumps in front of Snow. *Idiot.*

"What am I going to do?" I ask the others.

Ollie presses his lips together. "Maybe if you hit Harlow, you'll break the spell." I look at him like he's nuts. "Hey, it's worth a shot."

Harlow starts to chant the way Jocelyn did in detention, and I realize I'm out of time. Harlow releases the arrows, and they fly through the air. With no other options, I take off at a run with my sword in my hand, praying the thing doesn't slice me as I go.

Harlow turns to me at the last moment, and I see the swords change direction.

"Gilly!" Maxine screams just as I dive to the ground and slide as hard as I can into Harlow, knocking her straight off her feet. I cover my head as swords rain down on me, and then the world goes black.

Happily Ever After Scrolls

Brought to you by FairyWeb—magically appearing on scrolls throughout Enchantasia for the past ten years!

BREAKING NEWS:

Gargoyles Attack Fairy Tale Reform School on Royal Day!

by Beatrice Beez

The royal visit to FTRS ended in a near-disaster today when gargoyles broke into the school and placed Professor Harlow under a spell to do their bidding. "Gargoyles appeared in this crazy purple cloud. Everyone was shrieking. It was insane. Cool, but insane, dude!" said Ollie, a student. "I was scared," another student, Maxine, told us. "I thought Harlow was going to destroy the princesses—and us along with them. She probably would have if Gilly didn't break the spell."

Gillian Cobbler, the village shoemaker's daughter and a newcomer to FTRS, came to the rescue. Harlow was magically forced to throw swords at the princesses and captured students. She is said to have come out of the spell after young Gilly knocked her to the ground. The professor is resting comfortably in her chambers and regrets what happened. "Those gargoyles will pay," she said in an official statement.

"Gilly's quick thinking stopped the gargoyles from hurting us," said Princess Rose, who was slightly injured in the attack. "Ella and I are grateful to this commoner for her heroic act."

Sources tell us that Rose and Ella are none too pleased about FTRS's lack of security. How were the gargoyles able to get on the school's grounds? Who sent them? Were they responsible for all the incidents that occurred throughout the day? One of Madame Cleo's tanks exploded during a dancing observation (no one was hurt, but they were quite wet), and a botany class turned ugly when a peony ant attacked.

We have to wonder: Could students be behind all these misdoings? "Is FTRS reforming students the way it claims to be?" asked a palace source privy to details inside the attack. "Or are these dark doings happening because villains are running that place?"

It's no wonder there is growing concern about security for the much-anticipated FTRS Ball that was officially announced on Royal Day. Plans were to hold the ball next week. "The dwarf squad and Snow White are going over everything that happened and will let us know whether it is safe for the royals—or the community, for that matter—to attend the anniversary ball," said a palace source when asked for comment. "We're also looking into whether FTRS is a safe place for Enchantasia's troubled youth."

Requests to speak to Headmistress Flora about this matter were denied.

CHAPTER 14

Rotten Apple

"Ah, Miss Gillian. Come in, come in!"

For a moment, I'm pretty sure I must be in the wrong place.

The Evil Queen is smiling—*cheerily*—and waving me into her office.

I clutch the note given to me when I was released from the infirmary this morning.

Miss Gillian Cobbler—Please be so kind as to join me for a meeting in my office this morning at ten sharp!

Sincerely, Professor Harlow

I was sure Jax had left me the note as a joke, but the nurse said it was legit. "He checked on you twice while you were out cold," said the gnome in the bright-blue nurse scrubs whose badge said Natasha, Gnome Nurse Level 1. "Aldo kept watch over you too when your friends weren't here."

That was creepy.

"I don't see a Kayla on the visitor sheet," Natasha said when I asked about my roommate. "I only see Jax, Ollie, and Maxine. You didn't wake up for days! That was some nasty bump you got on your head."

"Maybe Kayla was admitted," I wondered aloud. She had been acting odd in the gym. Kayla could have been ill.

Natasha shook her head, and her pointy hat nearly fell off. "No Kayla on my list, but you got a lot of get-well flowers." She grinned, and I noticed she only had four teeth. "You're like a celebrity in this school! Saving the royal court like you did."

I was only trying to rescue Jax. I wasn't sure how my honesty would go over with Natasha, so I kept quiet and looked at my flowers. The bouquets next to my bed were so big they could have been trees. The elaborate topiary shaped like a crown could only have come from the princesses, and the note attached confirmed it.

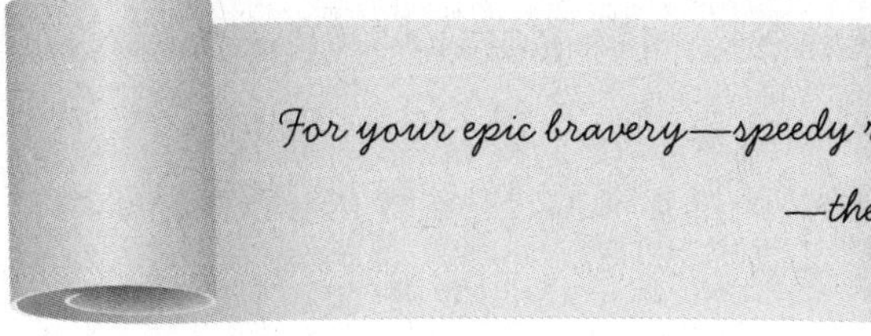

There was a small bouquet from my family and a few other handpicked arrangements, one with squished flowers that I assumed Maxine picked with her less-than-dainty troll hands. My head felt too heavy to read all the note cards. Natasha said I was hit with a bunch of the steel swords that rained down from the sky. My arms and legs were nicked up too. "You're lucky one didn't lop your head off!" Natasha said as she changed my bandages one last time. "Professor Harlow lost her pinkie in the mess and had to charm it back on."

Professor Harlow beckons me to her desk with her bandaged hand. While I'm in hospital clothes (a tee and baggy pants), my professor is back to wearing one of her formfitting velvet gowns. Aldo leaves the Evil Queen's shoulder and swoops across the room, startling me when he takes a perch on my arm. I wince as he sinks his claws into one of my bandages.

Professor Harlow chuckles—chuckles! "Aldo, I know you're happy to see Miss Cobbler, but leave her be. She's still recovering. How do you feel, child?"

"Okay." I feel like I've dropped into a different land with this conversation.

Maybe she's happier in her office than in her classroom. This room is brighter with all the torches and mirrors of every size and shape along one lavender wall. There is an inviting purple velvet armchair near her fireplace, which has a mantel full of self-help books above it, and on the other wall is a vanity table with lots of bottles and beauty products. I notice the gold mirror she keeps in a glass case has been moved to her office, along with Aldo's jeweled cage. The Evil Queen sits behind her desk, peering at me fondly.

So weird.

"I'm sorry I've asked you to come straight from the infirmary," Harlow says, "but this matter could not wait." She smiles, her deep purple lips curving up in the corners of her heavily made-up face. "I brought you here this morning so I could personally thank you."

I almost fall out of my chair, which, I should add, is so low I have to look up at Harlow's desk. I wonder if she has it set that way on purpose. "Come again?"

"Not only did you save the princesses, but you also saved me from once again becoming the Evil Queen." Harlow gives me a rare smile. "My sister would be an orphan right now if you hadn't stopped me from hurting anyone on Royal Day, and for that, I thank you."

As with Natasha, now might not be the time to bring up how I was only trying to save Jax. Everyone else was just a happy coincidence. "You're welcome?" I question. I've never heard the professor thank anyone for anything before.

"That's why I brought you here right from recovery. I wanted to be the first to commend you for your selfless act of bravery. We'd be reading a very different type of scroll this week if you had not broken the bewitchment I was under."

I lean forward, intrigued. Natasha saved some of the old scrolls for me to read when I woke up. She said it would be easier for me to understand what had happened the last few days if I read it myself. "Do you know who cast the spell or sent the gargoyles? Why were so many events sabotaged on

Royal Day? Do you think Gottie is behind this? Mr. Harking did go missing and so did his family…"

Harlow's face darkens. "I see no point in playing guessing games, Miss Cobbler," she snaps. "Rest assured, Headmistress Flora is working with the staff to figure out who is behind these acts and who could have bewitched someone as powerful as me."

That's another thing I didn't think of. Who could put a spell on the Evil Queen?

Harlow twirls a long, gold amulet that hangs from her neck. "That is why Headmistress Flora is not at our meeting today. She, Cleo, and Wolfington have asked me to speak on their behalf."

"Speak on their behalf?" I suddenly feel uneasy.

Squawk! Aldo seconds my confusion.

The Wicked Stepmother is the one who runs this school. She's the one who sent my enrollment notice and escorted me to detention. If I have to deal with someone here, I want it to be her.

"You're not in trouble, Miss Cobbler." Harlow adjusts her tiara, which has been slightly tilted since I walked in. "On the contrary. I have good news to share. While you have only served two weeks—three if you count the almost week you've been in the infirmary—of your required stay here, your bravery shows you're more reformed than any of us realized. Only someone who is truly thinking of others could have done what you did. Therefore, Flora and I would like to offer you an early release from the program."

I feel like someone just pulled my chair out from under me. I jump up. "Seriously?"

"You get to go home," my professor translates. "Immediately."

This doesn't make any sense. "But Headmistress Flora said—"

"I know what Flora said." Harlow's voice tightens. "You've flunked out of Fairy Tale Reform School, so to speak, and that's a good thing!" She laughs, but it sounds fake. "I've already sent a scroll to your parents letting them know they can pick you up."

My heart starts to speed up. I'm going home? Today?

"Unfortunately, your parents are out of town for a few days at a shoemakers' convention, but they said they will come straight home and should be here by Friday afternoon."

"The day of the FTRS Ball?" I question. Natasha filled

me in on the ball's will-they-or-won't-they-let-the-school-have-it gossip.

Professor Harlow's smile widens. "Why, yes. I didn't think you'd care about something as silly as a ball when you could go home to Hamish, Han, Trixie, Felix, and Anna."

I squirm. I don't like that she knows their names, but I'm desperate to see them. "So you mean they're still having the FTRS Ball even after everything that happened?" I ask. "But what about security? The *Happily Ever After Scroll* this morning said—"

"I know what the scroll said!" Harlow's voice booms, and the torches in her room dim. Aldo rushes into his cage, and I watch the look on my professor's face twist into something sinister. But then just as quickly, the room brightens and the Evil Queen is smiling her awkward smile. "I just mean, we are well aware of the scroll exaggerations. A ball is happening, and I will be releasing a statement later today telling all of Enchantasia they have nothing to fear in attending. Really, Miss Cobbler. You've done enough to help our school and me." Harlow offers Aldo a small treat, and he nips it out of her hand. "Go home to your family and enjoy your life."

Madame Cleo's prediction flashes in my mind, but I

quickly push it away. Professor Harlow is right. I can't worry about what's happening at FTRS or Jax, Kayla, Ollie, or Maxine. They'll survive. They'd ditch me if they had the chance to leave. My family is more important. Anna hasn't written, which means she's still mad or hungry or desperate. I think of Han crying out in hunger, and I want to race right out of the Evil Queen's office. My loyalty is to them.

I'm a thief, plain and simple, and I belong at home. Not in Fairy Tale Reform School.

"Now if you'd just sign these forms." Harlow slides a long, wordy scroll across the desk to me along with a black-feathered quill. I try to read the words, but they're too tiny. "Just customary release paperwork, of course, saying you are never again permitted to cross school grounds or converse with students in our care."

That's a weird clause to have in reform school release papers. I sign them anyway.

"Good girl! Excellent!" Harlow folds her hands in her lap and flashes me a questionable smile. "You'll forget all about this place in no time."

Chapter 15

Right, Wrong, and In Between

There she is!" Maxine cries as I walk into the cafeteria for what will be my second-to-last dinner there. "FTRS's hero!"

Me? A hero?

I never thought someone would use that word to describe me, but here I am holding my dining tray, and several hundred students of every kind are suddenly applauding and cheering for me. The sound echoes through the room with high ceilings and fish tanks. The left side of the room is less rowdy (Have you ever seen an ogre eat? Not only are they messy, but they break their plates at every meal!), and that's where I find my friends cheering the loudest. Maxine, Ollie, and Jax wave me over to a round table piled high with food.

"We're so happy you're okay," Maxine says, squeezing me a little too tightly and making one of my bandages pop off. "Oops! Sorry. Want me to get your dinner for you? You sit right here." She practically throws me into my seat. "What do you want?" She waves her large, hairy hand away. "No matter. I'll get you everything! You need your energy if you're going to be ready for the FTRS Ball."

For a split second, my heart sinks. Maxine and I were talking last week about what we were going to wear to the ball. Jax had offered to practice a few steps with me, and Ollie even said he'd escort Maxine and me personally. Now I won't be here.

"Did you hear they got Gnome-More for the band?" Ollie asks us. "Goblins of Fire got spooked when they heard what's been going on." He waves a turkey leg around. "Can't say I blame them. The way this place is going, I wouldn't be surprised if the whole party went up in flames. Good thing we have Gilly here to save us again."

I feel my body stiffen. Ollie's making a joke, like he always does, but Madame Cleo's premonition hangs over my head. I look at my new friends' smiling faces, and I don't know how to tell them I'm bailing.

You're overthinking things, Gilly, I tell myself. *They'll understand.*

As Maxine heads off to get my dinner and Ollie goes back for seconds, Jax moves his chair closer to mine. I can smell the lavender hand soap he must have washed up with. I've never been so happy to see him. "You okay?" he asks. "Ollie was just joking."

"I'm a little tired," I lie. Now I'm lying to Jax too, and that makes me feel the worst of all. "Where's Kayla, by the way?"

Jax's face clouds over. "I've barely seen her since Royal Day. Maxine tried to get her to visit you, but Kayla said she was sick. Something is definitely going on with that girl. Have you talked to her?"

I shake my head. "She wasn't in our room when I got back there this afternoon." She didn't even leave a "welcome back" message or a note on our magic chalkboard. I guess Kayla won't miss me when I'm gone.

"So I owe you again, thief," Jax says with a smile. "Thanks for keeping me from getting killed."

"Well, I couldn't leave you hanging out all day in a bubble, even if it looked like you were trying to save the royals," I tease. Jax doesn't say anything. I lean in so no one can hear me. "I feel kind of bad that I'm getting the rock star treatment though. Everyone is acting like I saved the school when really I was just trying to save you! Even Professor Harlow thanked me." Jax's eyebrows go up. "She gave me early dismissal for my bravery. I'm out of here on Friday."

"You've been sprung?" he whispers, taking a bite of his fig pudding before he tucks in to the roast pheasant we're having tonight. Fairy bus girls fly between tables bringing extra napkins and condiments and clearing dirty dishes. Everyone is smiling at me, except Jax. "How? You've only been here for three weeks."

My chest tightens. "Professor Harlow says I've proven myself."

"You don't find anything strange about that?" Jax asks. "In my whole year here, the Evil Queen has never let anyone leave early for good behavior. Now she picks you, a girl who's fought with her sister, to let go home before the ball? Why?"

I close my eyes to block out the laughter in the room and the sound of tinkling silverware hitting copper plates. "I don't want to think about her reasons," I snap. "I don't care what happens here. I just want to go home. My family needs me." I open my eyes and look at Jax's serious face.

"Did you ever think this family needs you too?" Jax asks quietly.

"I don't want to listen to this." I push my chair back from the table and stride out of the room. I hear Jax calling me, but I don't turn around. When I reach the hallway, he catches up and grabs my arm.

"You and me? We've got to talk," he says gruffly and starts pulling me by the arm down a new hallway that appears in front of us.

"I don't care what you have to say," I protest, wincing as he touches one of my bandages by accident. "I've got to go pack!"

"You own three things. It won't take long." I've never heard him talk to me like this before. I'm so dumbfounded that I let him walk me straight to a bookcase, and I watch as he feels around for something among the self-help tomes. *Witchy No More*, *The Only Spell You Need Is Love*, *A Warlock's Guide to Bettering Yourself*, and Anna's favorite book, *No One Keeps Me in a Tower*, a guide to breaking out by Rapunzel herself. Jax pulls *Life Lessons from the Bog* forward slightly, and the whole bookcase moves back to reveal a garden courtyard in the middle of the castle.

"Whoa," I say as Jax pulls me inside. This must be where

the cafeteria grows fresh herbs and vegetables. I'm not surprised they've kept it hidden. Some of my classmates have an insatiable appetite. He closes the bookcase behind us. My nose smells basil and mint growing among the radishes, tomatoes, and cabbage.

Jax turns toward me. "I brought you here so we can talk without anyone overhearing." He takes a deep breath. "There's something you need to know before you bail, and I'm only telling you because I know I can trust you." His violet eyes glow in the dimming light. "I tried to keep you out of this, but you're too smart not to see what's going on right in front of you. You're a fighter, Gilly, and I could use someone like you on my side."

"On your side? What are you talking about?" He sounds crazy.

"That day we met, when I was breaking out of here—didn't you ever wonder why I didn't succeed? Why I made such an obvious mistake with the alarm?"

My smile vanishes.

"I needed it to look like I was trying to escape, but the truth is, I have reasons to stick around." Jax suddenly sounds much wiser. "I'm undercover."

I laugh so hard my belly hurts. "No, you're not." Jax doesn't crack a smile. I stop laughing. "You are?"

"For the royal family," he says simply. "I'm one of them, actually."

"*What?* You're not royal," I sputter. I can feel a lump forming in my throat. "You were raised on a farm. You said you ran away."

Jax plucks a sprig of basil off its vine. "That was part of my cover. This is a reform school. I needed people to believe I hated the royals and this school as much as anyone did, but the truth is, I'm actually Rapunzel's brother."

I feel my hands begin to tremble. He's one of *them*?

"We've long suspected there was a traitor in the castle," Jax tells me. "We've had too many close calls with the princesses to not think someone is feeding villains information."

"Villains?" Images of three possible people enter my mind. There's Gottie, Rapunzel's captor. (*Happily Ever After Scrolls* once posted what they claimed was a grainy picture of her and said the photographer was killed taking the image.) Alva, Sleeping Beauty's dragon of a witch, is the next baddie I imagine, but no one has heard from her in a decade. I bet she's even worse than Gottie. And then there is Rumpelstiltskin, the trickiest and most dangerous of them all. "You've heard Flora," I say. "No one's seen them in years."

"They're out there biding their time 'til they can rise again. Who do you think sent those gargoyles to the school? They're after something or someone at FTRS," Jax says, and I feel a chill go through my body. "We just don't know why. Are Flora or the other teachers working with them? Who was Flora meeting with that day we spotted her in the Hollow Woods? Is Harlow wicked again? That trance she was under was too perfect. Who could put the Evil Queen under a spell?"

Jax picks a piece of rosemary from its stem. "It was my father's idea to get someone close to the villains to learn what was up." He smiles. "What better place to do that than among thieves and crooks at FTRS? I've been getting myself in enough trouble to stick around without students getting suspicious for a year. It helps that I act like I don't care about anyone but myself." He grins. "I had you fooled, didn't I?"

I don't believe this. He tricked me! Now it makes sense—his expert dancing skills, royal name (Who has a name like

Jackson?), and the way he was up on royal doings. I thought we were friends, but friends don't keep secrets this big. "But you don't act royal! You're not spoiled. You're not selfish. You're not…royal!"

"We're not all made from the same shoe mold, Gilly." His violet eyes seem deeper somehow. "You should know that by now."

I hang my head shamefully, thinking of all the royal put-downs I've said in front of him. I feel like a fool. If Jax is royal and a totally great guy who gave up going to the Academy to hang out in a reform school to help his family, could I be wrong about other royals too? My head hurts at the thought. "If you're royal, don't people know you're Rapunzel's brother? The princesses didn't even give you a second glance on Royal Day. You let *me* save them."

"And my family is most grateful for that." Jax runs a hand through his hair, which is the color of corn. Like the corn I know now he obviously doesn't sow. "You saved me from blowing my cover. But no, the princesses don't know who I am. Before FTRS, I was away at boarding school since I was five. The princesses wouldn't recognize me if they tried, and Rapunzel, well, she had that whole locked-away-in-a-tower thing for a while. No one's seen me on royal grounds in years." He looks at me carefully.

"That's where you come in. I've been watching you the last few weeks. You've got the skills to get out of jams and fight fire with fire. You could help me stop the villains from the inside." I give him a look that could fry fish. "I'm serious!" he protests. "You're a royal hater. None of the teachers would suspect you of working with the royals."

No. Way. "I've got my own family to worry about. I could care less what happens to the royals."

"But don't you care what happens to *this* royal?" he asks quietly. "I thought we were friends."

Jax really thinks of me as a friend? It's been a long time since I've had one that isn't related to me. My family is all I've had for so long.

"You're not the first to hate me because of my title," he adds as a breeze makes the vegetables in the garden sway. "It doesn't say anything about who I am. I care about my family just like you do, and I want to stop these villains before they can destroy our kingdom."

"That's just it," I complain. "I can leave. This week! Get

out of here and go home where my family is safe. Why should I stick around and help you?"

"If you think they're going to stop at our school, you're wrong," Jax says darkly. "Even if you don't care about Kayla, Maxine, Ollie, or the other kids here, think of your family. They're not safe 'til we stop the villains."

Anna, Han, Hamish, Felix, and Trixie. Five reasons to go home immediately.

And five reasons to stay and help Jax fight.

"You're a thief. I am a liar. Think of all the kids in here we could get to help us. Never send a hero to do a villain's job." Jax grins mischievously. "This is a job for our kind, and you know it."

In Enchantasia, I wouldn't trust Jax as far as I could throw him. But inside FTRS, maybe who someone really is can be totally different from who you think they are. "Okay, let's say I decide to stay and help you for a bit—and I'm not sure if I am yet. Where do we start?"

Jax exhales slowly. "With your roommate."

"Kayla? Why?"

"You're a thief. Read the signs," Jax says. "Your roommate is hiding something, and I have a feeling it has to do with what happened on Royal Day. You saw how she fell apart in the gym. She knows who's behind it. I'm sure of it. How else would she know how to stop the gargoyles?" He grabs a fistful of radishes and shoves them in his pocket. "I think we can get through to her. We have to."

All the unexplained absences, the illnesses, how irritable Kayla gets. Maybe Jax has a point. "We're going to have to find her first. She wasn't in the dorm or at dinner. The Pegasi have been grounded since Royal Day. Where could she be holed up?"

"If I screwed up and didn't want to be found, I'd go to the last place anyone would expect to find me." Jax thinks for a moment. "What's the one class Kayla despises?"

"Stargazing," I say. "Maybe she's in the observatory."

"See that?" Jax beams. "You're helpful already." He steps out of the garden through the bookcase and beckons me back inside FTRS's treacherous walls.

I stare down the hall into the unknown, hoping for the best but expecting the worst. We've all done some pretty bad things to get thrown in here. Nothing as bad as plotting with a villain, but maybe Kayla is looking for a friend to dig her out of whatever mess she's in. Could that friend be me?

Jax and I make our way into the dome-shaped room a few minutes later. Outside, the sun is setting and the sky is a smattering of red, yellow, and orange. The room feels cold and the torches are unlit, giving the open space an eerie feel. Telescopes are set up near the windows. Star charts and maps are rolled up on empty chairs, and astronomy constellation charts hang on the walls like paintings. Scaffolding lines a wall where someone is installing extra magical security measures.

"Kayla? Are you in here?" Jax tries. "Gilly and I want to talk to you." Silence. Jax frowns.

I look up. A duct above us is missing a grate. I think of how Jax and I shimmied through one just like it that day we were caught by the gargoyles. "Maybe that's because she's up there." Jax's mouth breaks into a smile, revealing a dimple I never noticed near his left cheek.

"I like the way you think, thief." He rolls the scaffolding over to the hole in the ceiling and starts to climb. I follow. Within seconds we're at the top, peering inside the dark shaft. I can just make out a pair of loafers.

"Kayla?" I call. The shoes shift slightly. "We know you're here. Can we talk?"

"No." Her voice is hoarse.

"We'll wait you out," Jax tells her. "We have all night. We already locked the doorway where the duct lets out so that you can't become a flight risk." He winks at me.

Quick thinking.

I hear Kayla sigh and then the sounds of knees moving along the ductwork. When she nears, I see that her golden locks are particularly ungolden and dark rings frame her amber eyes. She extends a quivering hand, and Jax pulls her out. Her wings pop out and begin to flutter as the scaffolding shakes beneath us. She puts her hands out.

"Go ahead," she says. "Turn me in." Jax and I look at each other. "I know you've figured out what I'm up to." She looks at me accusingly. "Why do you think I've been avoiding you?"

If Kayla thinks we know exactly what she's done, maybe we can work this conversation to our advantage. "I've been on to you since the day I got here," I lie and hope Jax plays along. "We know you're behind the gargoyle attack and everything that went wrong on Royal Day."

A single tear plops down her cheek. "I didn't mean for anyone to get hurt," she surprises me by saying. "Gottie said she'd leave the kids alone."

Gottie. Jax glances at me. "If you fess up to us now, maybe we'll make sure Flora and the dwarf squad go easier on you."

Kayla nods sadly. "I know the world sees Gottie as the monster who kidnapped Rapunzel, but when I lost my family to Rumpelstiltskin, she was kind to me when no one else was. I'd been busted for flying without a license, illegal use of magic, and casting love spells on people who hate each other. People in my village didn't believe a word coming out of my mouth."

I think of what would happen to me in the same situation. Father may not adore me, but he wouldn't leave me out in the cold and no one in our village would either. "Tell us the truth—do you know why Rumpelstiltskin took your family away?"

Kayla grips the scaffolding tightly. "Because I asked him to." I'm momentarily stunned. "I didn't understand what I was doing, okay? I begged Rumpelstiltskin to get Mother to forget what I'd done so I wouldn't have to go to FTRS. I didn't know he'd wipe my family's memories clean so they couldn't even remember me." She looks away. "I should have known his help would come at a price."

"Rumpelstiltskin uses people to get what he wants," Jax says grimly.

"That's why I went looking for Gottie." Kayla wipes her nose with the sleeve of the gym shirt she's still wearing. "I knew someone with magic that powerful had to be able to break Rumpelstiltskin's curse." Her wings flutter slightly. "When I found her, it was as if she was expecting me. She offered me shelter and a warm meal, and she tried to help me.

"She said if I agreed to go to FTRS and act as her mole, then she'd find a way to break my contract with Rumpel. I've been trying to please her ever since." Kayla looks at me mournfully. "I was only trying to get my family back," she cries. "I didn't mean to hurt anyone. That's why I was always trying to help you escape, Jax. I thought I could get the people closest to me away before anything bad happened."

"And I made a good cover," I say, realizing it. "Flora was on to you. By taking the new girl around, you could show up in more places without anyone noticing, right?"

"Yes," Kayla admits, and her cheeks turn beet red. "But even if you were here when Gottie's plan went down, I wouldn't have let her hurt you. I swear!"

"Just like you didn't mean for her gargoyles to attack me

and Jax or for all of us to almost get killed in the gym," I point out.

"I knew you'd be okay. Gottie doesn't have the strength to cast a spell as big as the one she wants to do yet." Kayla's wings flutter faster. "That's why she needs Harlow and the others to work with her. She's been trying to turn Harlow since I got here. I think she's succeeded. But the others, I don't know. She doesn't give me many details."

"What do you mean she's not strong enough?" I ask.

"She wants to wipe everyone in Enchantasia's memories clean," Kayla explains. "If she and whomever she's working with cast that spell, everyone will believe the villains rule the kingdom. The royals will disappear when she burns down the school," she says hoarsely. "She wanted to do it on Royal Day, but Gilly screwed that up." Kayla looks at me. "She knows who you are now."

My family. My boot. Jax was right. I could run, but I couldn't hide for long if Gottie was really coming for us. I had to help. "How can we stop her?"

"Gottie's consumed with making the curse happen at the ball because the royal court will be together," Kayla tells us. "She's not going to fail twice, which is why she's so desperate for inside help. She's already gotten to Harlow. Her hope is to turn Flora next. I don't know if she has, but she's met with Wolfington. If she turns him, Cleo will follow, and then they'll have a team so powerful no one can stop them."

"We can."

I look down. Maxine and Ollie are standing at the bottom of the scaffolding.

"We've been trailing you since the vegetable patch," Ollie calls up to us. "I did a card trick with one of the cafeteria fairies while Maxine stole her key to the hallway you guys went down that locked behind you." He points to Jax. "Dude, why didn't you tell me you're royal? I've been dying to meet your sister!"

"You're royal?" Kayla freaks.

Jax narrows his eyes at Ollie and begins to climb down. "How'd you hear that?"

Maxine points to her oversized troll ears. "These babies are supersonic. How do you think I made coin selling gossip to *Happily Ever After Scrolls*?" Her good eye looks down. "Well, until they caught on that I was making half the stuff up."

So that's why Maxine's in this joint!

"We won't tell anyone." Maxine smiles lopsidedly. "As long as you let us help."

"Dude, I'm a genius at making weapons out of curtain rods." Ollie bounces up and down. "Let me help you kick some gargoyle booty!"

Jax is way more serious. "This is not going to be easy. We're going up against the biggest baddie in Enchantasia and possibly all our teachers. Gottie won't care that we're just kids. If we screw this up, we're toast."

Ollie is the first to put his tiny fist in the circle. "Then we'd better be ready to fight. Who's with me?" Jax throws his hand on top of Ollie's. Maxine and Kayla quickly follow. They look at me. Seeing Kayla's hand makes me hesitate for a moment.

But I have to remember: this is so much bigger than my feelings about Kayla. Finally, I join them. "As Harlow likes to say, keep your friends close. Keep your enemies even closer. Let's do this thing."

Happily Ever After Scrolls

Brought to you by FairyWeb—magically appearing on scrolls throughout Enchantasia for the past ten years!

BREAKING NEWS!

The Fairy Tale Reform School Ball Is ON!

by Beatrice Beez

An FTRS anniversary bash seemed out of the question after Royal Day, but we couldn't have been more wrong!

"An anniversary ball is happening, and all of Enchantasia is invited," Headmistress Flora told us exclusively. "We refuse to let our fears get in the way of celebrating five years of success." The headmistress has enlisted the popular gnome band Gnome-More to play and is catering the event with the Catch of the Day. "I tell our students the best way to fight fear is to face it straight on, and we intend to do that," says Flora. "This will be the most exciting ball Enchantasia has seen."

While the castle would not comment, our sources tell us the princesses will attend. "They're not happy that Flora is going ahead with plans, but what can they do?" said an anonymous source inside the castle walls. "Having the royals be no-shows would send a bad message to Enchantasia. Flora has pretty much pushed them into a corner on this one."

The headmistress says security will be tight, and the school is in the process of installing new protection charms, including the As You Wish 3000, one of the strongest charms to be used by a public institution. Guests will be limited to three hundred, so get to FTRS's gates fast if you want to secure a seat!

UPDATE at 3:25 PM:

The castle has confirmed the princesses *will* be in attendance at the FTRS Ball! "We agree with Headmistress Flora that fear is never an option," said Princess Snow in an official statement. (Hmm...usually these statements are made by Ella. Could she be ruffled by this FTRS news?) "As always, we support Headmistress Flora in her endeavors and are proud of all FTRS has achieved. We would be honored to be the first RSVPs." According to the school spokesmirror, 245 requests for invitations have already been logged. Get to their gates *now* if you want one of the remaining 55 invites!

Chapter 16

There's No Place Like Home

Miss Gillian Cobbler—Your parents will be arriving to pick you up in FTRS's great hall Friday at 1:00 p.m. sharp! Please gather your things and meet them there. Thank you for your stay at Fairy Tale Reform School.

—Professor Harlow

At 1:00 p.m. sharp, I walk to the FTRS lobby to meet my parents. I've rehearsed what I'm going to say to them a thousand times, but I'm still nervous. If Professor Harlow or Headmistress Flora is there to escort me out, then my plea to stay will never work. Thankfully, when I get to the lobby, I don't see either of them. The place is bustling with the elf and fairy cleaning crew who are hanging anniversary banners with the school crest, dusting statues, and making everything sparkle. I can hear Miri issuing commands from a jeweled mirror over the fireplace. "You missed a spot on that clock! Fluff the rug again. Do I see dust flying? I shouldn't see dust flying at all."

I nearly take out an elf lowering a banner that says "*Snow* Your Appreciation for the Princesses!" Maxine bragged about making it in art.

"Careful!" The elf swats at me with a feather duster.

"Sorry!" I walk hurriedly past him to avoid being seen by Miri and almost bump into my parents at the front doors.

"Gillian!" Mother throws her arms around me, and I drink in her familiar leather scent that I've actually begun to miss. "Are you okay?" She touches my head and examines my still-bandaged arms for signs that I'm not actually broken. "When we saw the *Happily Ever After Scroll* about Royal Day, we were so worried."

"I'm fine," I say, feeling worse now that Mother is standing right in front of me. "How is everyone?" I'm afraid to say my siblings' names out loud because it will just make what I'm about to say even harder. *I'm not coming home.*

Someone throws their hands over my eyes. "Surprise!"

"Anna?" I sputter. My sister uncovers my eyes, and I see she is standing in front of me in a cobbler uniform resembling my mother's. She looks taller than she did a few weeks ago (is that possible?), and I can smell her Rapunzel hair perfume. ("It sparkles and smells great! Just like me!" Rapunzel says in the ad.) Around her neck, Anna has the tiny locket I stole—I mean *got*—her for her last birthday. "What are you doing here?"

"Anna was so proud. She couldn't wait 'til you got home to see you!" Mother says as my sister dances around me. "The others are home planning a big hero's welcome at the boot. Felix, Hamish, and Han are already making signs, and Trixie…" Mother laughs. I can't recall the last time I heard her do that. "Trixie started to make you a cake even though we were out of eggs and…" She touches my cheeks with both hands. "You've only been here three weeks and already you're changing."

I glance at Father. He puts a hand on my shoulder and gives it a squeeze. I can't remember the last time he did that. "We're proud of you, Gillian."

Whoa. I don't think Father's ever said those words to me in my entire life.

My cheeks color as I think of the words "hero," "proud," and "party" being used about me. Thieving got me riches, but I've never received praise like this before. I don't know what to say.

"Did you really save Sleeping Beauty?" Anna asks excitedly, her cocoa-colored eyes shining. "I've been telling all my friends at trade school! You're going to be practically royal in the village. Tell us exactly what happened and don't leave out a word."

My family looks at me expectantly, but I can't lie to them like I have to others. "It wasn't really a big deal."

Father is watching me closely.

"It's a *huge* deal!" Anna says, squeezing my hand. She hasn't let go since she got here. "Why don't you seem excited? You're coming home today!"

This is what I wanted. To get home to my siblings, to make Anna proud, to get some respect from Father. And yet, none of this praise feels exactly right, and that is why I know now more than ever that I'm doing the right thing.

Mother frowns. "Gillian, where is your suitcase? Didn't you pack? Your professor said we needed to leave the grounds immediately because they're doing final preparations for the ball tonight."

I plant my feet firmly on the oriental rug under my feet and take a deep breath. This is much harder to say with Anna hanging on me. "I didn't pack because I'm not leaving today."

Mother looks baffled. She shows me the release scroll. "But it says here we can take you home. Professor Harlow said—"

"I know what Professor Harlow said," I say gently as Anna's face deflates, "but I can't go home just yet." I eye Miri's glowing mirror in the corner. "I'm sorry you closed the shop and had to make the trip over here, but there are things I have to do before I'm released, and they could take a while. Dark things are happening in Enchantasia," I say quietly, "things I can't talk about now, but I'm trying to help stop them. Others are too. People in here are depending on me," I say, being cryptic. "I wouldn't feel right if I left them now when they need me more than ever."

Anna drops my hand. "We need you!" she yells, her voice full of disappointment. I feel a pang. I can't even look at Father. "Mother has papers that say you can go home! We don't have enough to eat, and I don't know how to pluck from royals like you do. My first attempt failed."

"Anna!" Mother says in shock, and my heart sinks. What have I taught my sister?

"Anna, don't become a pickpocket like me," I tell her. "Just because the royals are easy to steal from doesn't mean it's right." Father looks at me with a note of pride.

Anna, however, is furious. "What has this place done to you? Now you think you can stop villains too? I don't know who you are. Mother, if she's not coming home, then I can't even look at her. I'm waiting outside." She stomps out the front doors before I can stop her. I'm not sure I would reason with her even if I could.

Anna, please forgive me, I think. *I'm doing this for you.*

"Gillian, you're not making any sense," Mother says, waving the scroll in her hand. "How can you stay when they want you to leave? I don't think I can just leave you here to help your little friends. We have an order."

My heart sinks. I know she's right, but I can't bail now.

I hear a ripping sound and look up. Father has surprised Mother and me by tearing the scroll to pieces. "I don't see any release scroll," Father says, and Mother's jaw drops. "I say she stays right where she is." Father touches my chin. "Staying here means a lot to you, doesn't it?"

"Yes, I'm trying to do something good, Father," I say, my voice wavering.

"Then I think you should," he says with a small smile. "You obviously have more work to do at Fairy Tale Reform School. Stay and make us proud."

"I will." I throw my arms around him and squeeze. I don't know when, if ever, I've hugged him, but he deserves a hug now. I'm not going to let my family or anyone inside these walls down.

Chapter 17

Let's Get This Party Started

When I sneak into the ballroom with Maxine a few hours later, I momentarily panic.

"Come on! Come on!" Maxine says, tugging on my arm because I've suddenly gone statue-like on the main staircase. "Let's go blend in before someone spots you."

I can't help myself. I'm blown away. I can't believe this is the same room where we practice dragon slaying. (We do *not* use a real dragon. Madame Tilly just conjures up a fake one for fire-safety reasons.) I've never been to a ball before, so I don't have a lot to go on, but I can't imagine anything as beautiful as this room. An intricate display of peonies, roses, gardenias, and ivy blankets the ballroom ceiling, which glows like stars thanks to lightning bugs and glowworms hanging out in it.

One wall is made of glass, revealing the largest aquarium I've ever seen. Madame Cleo and the mer-students are having their own party inside. The Sea Siren is wearing a glittery shell top, and her long hair is piled high on her head in an updo adorned with shells and starfish. She sways to the music before she is pulled into a dance by a mer-man who looks a lot like the one she danced with in detention.

A flash of lightning brightens the tables surrounding the dance floor where footmen and maids—usually busy laundering smelly socks and checking our mail for illegal objects—are carrying plates of roast lamb and cranberry salad. The number 5, for our school's anniversary, is everywhere. It's on table cards and banners, and has even been shaped into rolls.

Despite what some of the soggy guests around me are whispering as they come in out of the rain this late fall day, nothing was stolen for the festivities.

"You've got to give props to Headmistress Flora for going out with a bang," says Ollie when we find him bopping along to the band near the appetizer table. "I'm glad I dressed up." He's wearing a white pompadour and a blue suit that makes him look like a South Pole elf, and his hair is so shiny and slick I could ice skate on it.

"You can't even tell I have magic tricks hidden in this jacket." He slides his coat back to reveal a flower that squirts water, two decks of cards, and silver cuff links—I haven't a clue what he'd do with those. "I think we're ready to party!"

By "party," Ollie means battle. We've spent the last two days listening to Kayla tell us everything she can about Gottie, which isn't much. ("She's very dark and mysterious," Kayla said, which was less than helpful.) Ollie has stolen every radish in the school garden to handle the gargoyles, much to the gnome cafeteria chef's dismay. I just passed a flyer in the hall that said "Do You Know the Radish Thief? Reward for Information!"

I swiped a copy of Flora's scroll from her office, which had the party timeline—from princess arrivals to her speech. We looked it over in the Pegasus stables one afternoon, but to be honest, I couldn't find anything fishy. Jax struck out too. He tried to get word to the castle about what we think Gottie has planned, but with security so tight, we don't even know if they got Jax's message.

"I think we're on our own," he said grimly late last night when we were going over details one last time in the observatory, which has become command central. "Help might not be coming."

We're as ready as we'll ever be to try to stop our villainous teachers and one of the biggest baddies to ever hit Enchantasia.

And we're not all that ready.

If I think about what we're trying to do too much, I want to throw up in one of the emerald green vases near the punch station.

I catch Ollie staring at Maxine and me appreciatively. "You ladies clean up well."

"Thanks!" Maxine has a fondness for Chef Raul's gingersnap cookies, but in her hot pink dress and numerous accessories (three necklaces and a dozen pearl earrings in her pointy ears), she looks sweet. "I did Gilly's and my hair. Rapunzel gel will make it stay put even during an explosion."

Long curls drape down my back. When I try to shake my hair helmet from side to side, my curls barely move. "It's definitely a change from my ponytail," I say. "So is this dress." Ollie stole me the green taffeta gown from who knows where. It feels heavy and is hard to move in, but the hoop skirt is a great place to hide my radish supply. I tried to pinch us swords during gym, but I think Madame Tilly was on to me. I'm weaponless. We all are.

"Why do I think you're wearing shorts under that skirt?" Ollie asks.

"Because I am." I can't imagine this skirt doing me much good if we have to run. Better to be prepared, which is why I have bloomers on underneath. My eyes scan the room for signs of anything amiss. The dwarf squad is patrolling and doing random bag checks. If Pete knows I'm not supposed to be here, he hasn't said anything. A fairyographer is whipping up pictures. Headmistress Flora is watching the clock. Nothing seems out of the ordinary. *Yet.* "Have you seen Jax and Kayla?"

"Nope!" Ollie grabs Maxine's hand, just as Gnome-More starts playing a dance number. "Might as well dance and keep an eye on things on the floor."

Maxine turns to me and gives a silent squeal. "We won't go far."

I give her a small thumbs-up and watch them run down the stairs. A loud clap of thunder makes everyone freeze for a moment. It is nasty out. According to Miri, who gives us the weather every morning, "those who wear glass slippers instead of rain boots today are making more than just a fashion faux pas."

"Look at you, thief!" Jax comes up behind me with Kayla and walks around me. "I never thought I'd see you in a dress." He makes a face. "You stick out like a sore thumb in that thing."

I huff. "Well, you look royal in your outfit, so good job there." In a taupe silk jacket, cropped pants, and high socks, he looks like a prince, which I guess he is. "You look nice too, Kayla."

"Thanks," Kayla says in a small voice. Her shimmery dress is so pale blue it almost looks clear. Anna, a huge fashion fan, would definitely approve. Kayla keeps her eyes on the work boots that peer out from underneath my gown. "You too."

A flash of lightning brightens Jax's face. The rain is coming down so hard we can't see much of anything outside. "See anything unusual yet?"

"Wolfington was pacing the floor a few minutes ago, but other than that, all seems normal," I report. "Flora, Azalea, and Dahlia are talking to *Happily Ever After Scrolls*. Their reporters are stationed at every corner of the room. I haven't seen any sign of Harlow or Jocelyn though." And that makes me uneasy.

"Once the bait arrives, Gottie shouldn't be long after," Kayla says. "Or Harlow."

By bait, she means royals.

"I left the stables unlocked like she asked." Kayla's wings flutter more rapidly when she's stressed. "I still think we should have set up some magic there to stop her."

"I doubt one of Ollie's magic tricks could do that," Jax says grimly. "We're winging this thing."

"I'll double-cross her if I can," Kayla says. "We know I'm good at that."

Jax and I are quiet. Jax may be able to forgive Kayla for all she's done—it is the royal way—but thieves don't forget. I don't trust her.

"Evening, students." I freeze. Wolfington has somehow snuck up on us. He's wearing a green velvet suit, and his long hair is tamed in a ponytail. His blue eyes are unusually bright. "Miss Gillian, I'm surprised to see you here. How are you enjoying the ball?"

"I…" I look at Kayla and Jax, who are momentarily stunned. How could I have missed him in the crowd? "I decided not to go home," I blurt out. "I meant to go straight to the headmistress's office to let her know, but then I got sidetracked getting ready for tonight." I look down at my shoes. "I don't feel ready for Enchantasia yet."

Wolfington nods. "Quite understandable. We all have work we need to do before we return to our normal lives, don't we?" I blink rapidly. Did he hear me talking to my parents? "Personally, I'm glad you're staying, but if I were you, I'd stay out of Professor Harlow's way tonight." He takes a swig from the goblet in his hand. "She doesn't handle change as well as the rest of us, and I'd hate for her to spoil the party."

The three of us look at each other. "Yes, sir."

He scratches his chin. I can see his hair sticking out of his shirt cuff below his wolf cuff links. "You and your friends seem to have been preparing for this evening a lot. All those late-night chats you've been having in the observatory."

A bead of sweat forms on my brow. He's on to us. *Stay cool, Gilly. Deny, deny, deny.* Wolfington doesn't even give me a chance to do so.

"We just wanted to look our best, sir," Jax says calmly. "We needed to help Gilly find a dress since she changed her mind about staying at the last minute."

He eyes us all intently. "Well, you look wonderful. Enjoy your evening and do be careful," Wolfington says and disappears into the crowd.

"Oh my God." Kayla freaks. "What are we going to do?"

Suddenly Gnome-More stops playing and trumpets sound. A footman appears at the opposite staircase. "Hear ye! Hear ye!" he yells. "Presenting the Royal Court of Enchantasia—Princesses Ella, Snow, Rapunzel, and Rose!" The entire room seems to curtsy and bow at the same time.

The princesses are decked to the nines with tiaras, jewels, and dresses so big it seems almost impossible that they could sit down in them. They prove me wrong by heading straight to their table, which is surrounded by Snow's beloved dwarf squad. Maxine and Ollie make their way back, and the five of us peer out at the crowd, waiting for something to go wrong. Flora heads to a podium and begins to give a speech about our school's anniversary, and I feel my back go up.

Something is going to happen any minute now. I can feel it. But I'm wrong. Minutes later, Gnome-More is playing again, and a fairyographer is leaving with Flora and some of the princesses to pose for pictures in the entrance hall. Madame Cleo disappears from her tank, and I assume she's headed to the photo op as well.

"This might be the nicest ball I've ever been to," I hear a guest say as she passes by me. "Can you believe we're in a reform school? I hope no one tries to hurt us!" Her friend laughs.

But it's not funny. Someone wants to hurt all of us. I scratch my neck. I'm breaking out in hives. Where is Gottie?

Kayla begins to hyperventilate as people go back to dancing or head off to get food. "I don't understand. She should be here by now with her army of gargoyles. I swear!" she insists.

"Liar, liar," Jocelyn tsks, appearing out of nowhere. She grabs Kayla and me by the arms. "Kayla just doesn't want you to join the real party, but I do." Her smile fades. "All of you are coming with me."

CHAPTER 18

Playing by the Rules Is for Wimps

I thought you were smarter, Cobbler," Jocelyn says icily and flicks her annoying black cape so it billows out behind her. She's leading us down a hall away from the ballroom. She has a small purple mirror I recognize from Harlow's office pointed at our backs. She already warned us about trying to make a move to escape. "My sister gave you an out. You'd be home with Mommy and Daddy right now if you had just listened to her. Instead, you've made things much worse for you and your friends."

"I swear! I don't know what she's talking about," Kayla insists, whimpering as we're led along. "Gottie told me she was coming to the ball."

Jocelyn whirls around. "Do you really think she'd be so foolish as to show up in the middle of a room with all of

Enchantasia watching? Why do you think she sent her gargoyles to do her bidding on Royal Day?"

"I guess Harlow wasn't really under a spell that day, was she?" Jax asks. I watch him motion to Ollie to get something out of his jacket. He moves his hand slightly and Jocelyn's hands begin to crackle. She sends a zap Ollie's way, and he flinches.

"Don't be stupid. Harlow couldn't fall under a spell set by gargoyles," Jocelyn says. "She was trying to take out some of the royals for Gottie without having to bring the Wicked One into it." Jocelyn's dark eyes burn through me. "But you had to go and mess things up, and now I'm stuck delivering you five to her instead of staying out of things like my sister wanted."

"So don't do it," I say, stalling for time 'til I can figure out my next move. "You don't want to help someone like Gottie, do you?"

Jocelyn laughs. "What choice do I have? Even if we get out of this place, my sister and I will always be outcasts." For a brief moment, I can see the pain that realization gives her. "She'll never be forgiven for the things she's done, and I'll never be able to escape her legacy. So I say, why not have fun while I'm stuck here? Now move!"

She pushes Ollie and Maxine through a new hallway that has just popped up, and I see we're descending to the dungeon level that I've heard about but never seen. Why would I? Flora built this place to deal with criminals like Gottie, but she's never been caught. Torches illuminate our path down as the air grows colder and damp, and then we're standing in the middle of a large opening among half a dozen cells. Harlow is waiting for us.

She's in a gown and cape that glitter brighter than any of the princesses' outfits, and her pale face has flawless makeup that looks like it took hours to apply. Atop her head is the most elaborate black-jeweled crown I've ever seen. Jocelyn hands her sister the mirror, and the glass swirls gold and silver, crackling like lightning.

"Ah, Miss Gillian, I see you stayed and brought guests to watch the show," Harlow sneers. "Foolish girl. Now you'll burn with the rest of this school." With a flick of her wrist, Harlow pushes us into a corner, and we fall into a heap. "It's almost time for the main event. Upstairs, right above us actually, all of Enchantasia is dancing the night away, not knowing we're about to turn their minds into goo. They'll never remember themselves, let alone who runs this kingdom. Even if they could, the princesses will already be turned to ash."

"You'll never get away with this," Jax says.

"Oh, but I already have," Harlow says patronizingly. "Cleo is an ice cube in her aquarium, and Flora and the royal court are immobilized in the great hall. All that's left to deal with is you five—after I cast the spell." She holds the mirror up to the ceiling and lightning flies out of it, sending rocks down on our heads. A crack begins to spread above us.

"You're not strong enough to cast a spell that large," I challenge her.

Harlow drops the mirror for a moment. "I know that. That's why the Wicked One is here."

A bushy, gray-haired figure emerges from the shadows of one of the cells. She's flanked by two gargoyles that hiss when they see us. Jax begins to move our small group back. Gottie's face, up close, is hard to look at. Warts cover her skin like freckles. Her nose twists sideways in an awkward position, and her teeth have clearly never seen a toothbrush.

"Hello, darlings." Her full lips curl into a snarl. "Thank you, Kayla, for getting these nuisances out of the way."

"I didn't do anything!" Kayla cries. "You told me you were coming to the ball."

"And so I have, but even I wouldn't be foolish enough to

announce my arrival. Not when there are other ways into the room upstairs." Out of her pocket, she pulls a mirror that is identical to Harlow's and aims it above us. It shoots out more lightning that makes the crack above us widen. I close my eyes to keep from seeing people fall from the sky, but so far, nothing happens. "Once they're disposed of, I can rid myself of these horrid clothes." Gottie shrugs. "Or I could do that now. It's not like anyone up there will see me 'til after, and by then, they'll only know me as their queen."

A purple cloud of smoke surrounds her, and within seconds, Gottie's ragged clothes, wart-covered face, and white frizzy hair have disappeared. An older woman appears in her place wearing a gown as red as fire and a cape with a collar so high it could practically be a hood. Her jet-black hair is pulled back with a gold comb covered in what looks like dragons. She has the same symbol on the thick gold cuffs on her wrists and the long necklace draped around her thin neck.

Kayla gasps. "Alva?"

Alva laughs. "Yes, my gullible pet. Gottie and Alva are one and the same." She pulls Kayla toward her and whispers in her ear. "You were useful gathering the information that I needed, but now you've served your purpose." She opens a gate to a dungeon, and Kayla is flung through the air and dropped inside. The door shuts behind her. Kayla grabs the bars.

"I did everything you asked," Kayla stutters, her wings popping in and out. "You promised if I did, you'd help me, Gottie."

"Gottie's been dead for years, you fool!" Alva thunders. "I have allowed the world to think otherwise so I could plan my return without ever being spotted. I only needed a young fairy with thoughts as dark as yours to do my bidding, which you've done marvelously." She looks our way, and I cringe. "Not a soul is on to us, but these delinquents here."

So Rapunzel's captor has bit the dust and Sleeping Beauty's dream-maker, who no one has seen in an eternity, is pulling all the strings? Talk about being duped.

"It was all so easy. When Rumpel told me of your wishes, I knew you were the one I was looking for. I suggested that Rumpel make your family forget you, and he did." Her grin makes me feel cold. "I couldn't risk them remembering you at some point. That's why I eventually turned them all into hollow trees."

"*No!*" Kayla crumples to the floor of her cell. Anger builds up inside me as I watch Kayla sob.

"Yes!" Alva sounds like a snake. "They had to be taken care of, just like you all will be. And then *I* will rule Enchantasia, and the royals will burn." Within moments, Ollie, Maxine, Jax, and I are picked up and sent flying into the cell adjacent to Kayla. As soon as I drop, I make a run for the door, and Alva zaps me with her mirror. I try to move, but it feels like I'm stuck in molasses. And that's when Jocelyn is flung into the cell with us. She topples into Ollie and Maxine, knocking Maxine out cold.

"Alva, what are you doing?" Harlow's voice is shrill. "My sister has done nothing to harm your plan."

"She's a liability, just like they are," Alva says coolly.

"But—" Harlow moves toward her, and purple bolts shoot from Alva's hand.

"No buts or I'll dispose of you as well," Alva says. "I can do this on my own, or have you forgotten how you let me down the last time?"

Harlow hangs her head.

"Harlow!" Jocelyn races to the bars and rattles them, but Harlow does not look up. I see Jocelyn's lips start to move, and she begins to chant. I wonder if she'll be able to break through the bars that hold us. Alva notices and flings bolts toward the bars. Jocelyn goes flying back, falling into me.

"Stop bumping into me," I grumble, flinging her off me.

"It's no use," Jax says as Ollie cradles Maxine's head. Kayla rocks back and forth, seemingly oblivious to what's going on around her. "We can't break these bars."

We all watch as Alva gives her gargoyles instructions. She glances in her mirror, and I can just make out the tiny figures in the frame. They must be the royal court, which is being held upstairs with Flora. "Go! Check on them and make sure the magic is holding. After that we can begin the spell," she tells one of the gargoyles, and he flies off only to return moments later. "Grrr…that's true. You can't be seen. I'll do it myself. Harlow, watch them!" She points to Jocelyn. "*All* of them. If I return and she's not here…"

"Yes, Alva," Harlow says, but her voice sounds hollow.

Once Alva's gone, Harlow walks toward our cell, her eyes on Jocelyn. "I'm so sorry, sister." The remaining gargoyle paces in front of our cages.

Seconds later, I see a radish roll past me. Harlow peers at it curiously as the gargoyle snatches it. He gobbles it down and drops in a heap.

"That's one problem solved," Ollie says cheerily, opening his coat to reveal more radishes.

"Harlow, you know she can't complete the spell without both mirrors," Jocelyn says, shaking. There are purple bruises on her hands from where she's been hit by Alva's rays. "Give us yours."

"Your only shot would be to aim my mirror at hers and take both out, but she'll kill you before you can even raise your arm," Harlow says. "Besides, the minute she notices my mirror is missing…" Her face crumbles.

"Is there anything else we can use?" I ask.

"No, you fool!" Harlow snaps, whirling toward me. Any sympathy she has for her sister, she doesn't have for me. Her voice is full of rage, and the deafening sound sends rocks falling from the cracked ceiling. We shrink back. "If there was something I could use to get my sister out of here, don't you think I would have?"

Jax clings to the bars. "She's betrayed you the way she's betrayed everyone else. If you want to save your sister, you have to help us."

Ollie looks up from where Maxine lies. Her chest rises and falls so I know she's still breathing, but the bruise on her head looks ugly. "Maybe we could trick her. Give her a phony mirror."

"How are we supposed to do that, genius?" Jocelyn snaps.

"You could create one," I say, thinking aloud. "If you can

create a dance partner in detention, then you can make a lousy little gold mirror."

"You conjured up a dance partner?" Harlow asks, and her sister shrugs.

Jocelyn takes a deep breath and closes her eyes. Her lips begin to move, and I feel a sudden gust of wind. Moments later, a mirror that looks much like Harlow's is in Jocelyn's hands. I grab it and slide it into the poufy sleeve of my dress.

"Great. So you've got a mirror," Jocelyn says mockingly. "How are you going to get out of here, Cobbler, when my sister can't make that happen?"

"With my help." Wolfington walks into the light and Harlow steps back, preparing to do magic. "I think we have bigger problems at stake than you and me, don't you agree, Professor Harlow?" he asks calmly. "Save the magic for our bigger concern."

"How can you help, Wolfington?" Harlow says with a sigh.

Wolfington moves closer to our cage, ignoring her. "Students, we don't have much time. Whatever procedures we had in place to deal with Gottie or Alva are now null and void, thanks to Harlow."

"Not helping," the Evil Queen hisses.

"If Professor Harlow can't break you out, maybe I can break in, but it will be risky." Wolfington strokes his beard.

"You're not suggesting..." Harlow is flabbergasted.

"I am," Wolfington interrupts. "There's no full moon tonight, but if you help me turn into the Wolf Man, I can break through those bars. Once I do though, none of you will be safe." I shudder.

Jax smiles grimly. "It's the only shot we have. We have to take it."

Harlow looks at me. "You'll have seconds to take that phony mirror of yours and swap it with Alva's. You'll probably get yourself killed trying, but if it gives my sister a chance..."

"Please try, Harlow," Jocelyn says.

"Glad to see the Evil Queen hasn't gone soft under pressure," Ollie mutters.

Harlow looks at Wolfington. "Ready?" He nods. With a flick of her wrist, she produces a bottle of something blue and hands it to our professor.

He holds it up to us in a toast. "For luck," he says and then downs it in one gulp.

The transformation happens quicker than I would imagine, and Harlow hurries out of the way as Wolfington's clothes begin to tear, his hair begins to grow, and he falls to all fours before letting out a wolf howl that makes me shiver. When he looks up again, his eyes are yellow. We make eye contact for a moment, and then I hear him growl. His teeth begin to gnash, and we all move back. I can't believe I'm looking at the same person.

"Wolfington, think!" Harlow yells as he heads right toward her. With one furry hand, he swipes and the Evil Queen zaps him. It stuns him for a second before he lunges again, knocking her down. Jocelyn screams.

"Hey! Wolfie! Over here!" Jax yells, using a copper cup on the floor to bang on the bars. Wolfington stops and turns toward Jax.

All I can see is Harlow's mirror lying on the floor. If I can get to that mirror, I'll have more options when Alva returns.

"Everyone move!" Ollie says, pulling Maxine into a corner. Jax moves in front of her, and Jocelyn closes her eyes and begins to chant. Within seconds, a shield rises in front of them. The shield does not include me. Typical. Wolfington lunges and I dodge, sliding to the side as he barrels through the cage, breaking right through it. The Wolf Man lunges for the shield and gets shocked by electricity in the process.

Ah, now I see what Jocelyn's doing. I cringe, thinking of Wolfington hurt, but I can't worry right now.

"Harlow? What is going on down here?" Alva falters when she sees the Wolf on all fours. He springs toward her, and Alva holds out her mirror, zapping him to the floor.

That's when I make a break for Harlow's mirror, diving on top of it. Alva screams, and I take that moment to perfect the sleight-of-hand move I've used countless times in the village. I take the fake mirror out of my sleeve and place the real one inside it. Then I prepare to crunch the phony one with my work boot. "Take one more step and I'll break the mirror," I tell her. "You won't be able to cast the spell without it."

Alva begins to cackle. "You foolish child! That mirror is made from fairy's blood. It can't be broken by human hands." She uncurls her fist and places her palm up. "Give it to me." I hold the mirror tighter, feeling my heart beat inside my chest. "I have to do everything myself," she grumbles, and I feel the mirror fly from my hands to Alva's free hand.

I hold my breath and watch as the Wicked One caresses the mirror in her hands. Her eyes widen. "Why, you little thief!"

"Gilly, now!" Jocelyn screams, and I watch as she tries to put a shield up around me.

Sliding Harlow's mirror out of my sleeve, I aim it at the real mirror in Alva's other hand. A silver ray flies out before Alva can react. The connection causes an explosion that sends us both flying backward to the ground. The ground shakes, and large chunks of the ceiling begin to cave in. I feel slightly dizzy, and my ears are ringing. Above us, I can hear screaming. Alva stands back up, clutching her side, which is bleeding, and I worry I'm done for. I don't think I could get up right now if I tried. We lock eyes as we hear the sound of people and footsteps heading our way.

"Down here!" I hear Pete shout. Better late than never.

Alva's face may be bruised, her once beautiful hair may be singed, but her gaze doesn't falter as she stares at me, the thief who just beat her.

"This is far from over," she whispers and then with a *poof*, she's gone.

Happily Ever After Scrolls

Brought to you by FairyWeb—magically appearing on scrolls throughout Enchantasia for the past ten years!

BREAKING NEWS:

Enchantasia on High Alert! Alva Seen at FTRS!

by Beatrice Beez

Saturday's Fairy Tale Reform School ball ended in near disaster when the Wicked One herself, Alva, was said to be spotted in the school. "One minute everyone was dancing to our single, 'Gnome the One You're With,' and the next people were running for their lives," said Herbert Hughes, Gnome-More's lead singer, who broke his arm fleeing.

The school's ballroom floor did crack in half, but rumors of a wolf man have not been confirmed. "As soon as someone said Alva was there, everyone ran!" said Margo Menny, a troll from Galvington who had used her vacation money to see the princesses and instead left with one shoe and a broken handbag. "That wicked fairy is even more dangerous than Gottie!"

Sources tell *Happily Ever After Scrolls* that Gottie and Alva may be the same person, but we cannot confirm this news as of yet. All we know right now is that the dwarf squad is asking the community to be vigilant. "Lock your doors and if you see something unusual, say something," said Pete, chief of the Dwarf Police Squad.

While Headmistress Flora has yet to comment on what really happened at the ball, the royal court is preparing for battle. "If this truly is the work of Alva, we will bring her to justice," said Princess Snow.

The same goes for Professor Harlow, who was found to be working with Alva and is currently being held in the FTRS dungeons. The professor's younger sister, Jocelyn, was questioned and released.

Stay tuned to Happily Ever After Scrolls *for updates on the search for Alva!*

Pegasus Postal Service
Flying Letters Since The Troll War!

FROM: Anna Cobbler (2 Boot Way)

TO: Gillian Cobbler (Fairy Tale Reform School*)

*Letter checked for suspicious content

Gilly,

I don't understand you! When Mother and Father got word you were being released, I couldn't wait to go with them to pick you up. Han, Hamish, Trixie, and Felix were decorating for your welcome home party. How could you stay and let all of us down? Everyone was in tears when we came home without you.

Do you have any idea how hard things have been without you? Money is tighter than ever. Father lost business when people found out his daughter had been hauled off to FTRS. Mother took on a second job as a seamstress, but there's still not enough to get by. I thought we could hold on 'til your return, but I have no idea when that will be. And the only way I can talk to you is by scroll now that Enchantasia is on lockdown because of Alva. Thanks Gilly—for nothing.

Anna

Pegasus Postal Service
Flying Letters Since The Troll War!

FROM: Gillian Cobbler (Fairy Tale Reform School*)

*Letter checked for suspicious content

TO: Anna Cobbler (2 Boot Way)

Anna Banana,

Please don't be mad at me. Being stuck at FTRS has made me see that doing the easy thing is not always the right thing. It kills me to hear how hard life has been for you guys, but be strong. There has to be another way to get food. Ask Gnome-olia if you can work one afternoon after school and take home stale bread. Or talk to Combing the Sea about helping sell their Rapunzel line.

You're a natural salesperson! You even had me wanting her shampoo. Help Father think up an even cooler shoe than a glass slipper. Then everyone will be begging for his foot apparel!

In here, I've learned stealing can't be a career. That's why I have to stick around FTRS for a while. To learn what I'm good at so I can have a job to help you all when I get out. I was as selfish as a pixie before FTRS, but I promise next time you see me, you're going to be proud. That's something I want more than anything in this world.

Love, Gilly Bean

Chapter 19

The End or the Beginning?

It took almost a week for the FTRS crew to clean up the mess left behind by Alva. It took another for the students to be allowed to leave their dorm rooms unaccompanied by a teacher, which was tough since there wasn't enough staff left to cover the students. Harlow was in the dungeons. Madame Cleo was on a monthlong spiritual retreat near the Enchanted Sea. Professor Wolfington had disappeared. Most of the students I knew still didn't understand what had happened. They were rattled. And they hadn't had to fight Sleeping Beauty's tormentor.

It was time to get some answers, and there was only one person still around to give them: Headmistress Flora.

The day we were allowed to roam the halls freely again, we made a beeline for Flora's office. Painters and workers were still hanging new art, painting walls, and cleaning rugs. The area of the school near the ballroom was off-limits due to debris and unstable ground. For now, we were being schooled in the main building. Headmistress Flora insisted life get back to normal as quickly as possible.

But we all knew things were anything but normal.

"Come in," the Wicked Stepmother says when we knock on her door. "I was going to have Miri call you down so I could talk to you myself. Please, have a seat."

I haven't been in Flora's office since that day I stole a scroll to see what she had planned for the ball. Before that, I was there the day I arrived at FTRS. "I think I'll stand."

Flora nods. "Understandable." She threads her fingers together. "I believe you all have some questions for me." The five of us start talking at once. Flora holds up her hand. "Maybe I should go first," she suggests and runs a hand through the tight bun in her hair. "I assume you want to know if your teachers were working with Alva." The room is so quiet you can hear Maxine's patent leather shoes tapping. "Well, the answer is yes." Maxine inhales sharply. "Just not in the way you think."

Flora rises and steps around her desk, much as she did the day I arrived at FTRS. Her dark gray gown makes her look like she's in mourning. "We knew she had things planned for the royals and Enchantasia. We just didn't know what. We met with her when we could in the Hollow Woods, making it seem as if we were ready to join forces with her. Sadly, it seems Professor Harlow wanted to for real." She looks at me intently. "This was not a matter we wanted our students entangled in. Your safety is our utmost concern, and going up against Alva at the ball was foolish." She purses her lips. "That said, without you and Professor Wolfington, none of us might be here today."

"Are you going to tell *Happily Ever After Scrolls* how awesome we were?" Ollie asks eagerly, rubbing his arm where it was bandaged after Jocelyn's shield singed him. "Or pardon us and let us leave early like Harlow was going to do with Gilly?"

Headmistress Flora shakes her head. "I'm afraid that wouldn't be wise. Alva knows who you are now, and the safest place for you is here at FTRS with us."

Alva is coming for me. She pretty much said that. And no one I know is safe until she's taken care of. I think of how we fared against her when we worked together. Kayla's wings got damaged from Harlow's magic, and she won't be flyable for a while. Maxine got away with a slight concussion. I have some more nicks and bruises, and Jax had some rocks fall on him during the explosion and is on crutches. Still, we're alive.

"Have you heard from Professor Wolfington?" Maxine asks. "I always liked him, even if he did try to bite me in the dungeon."

Flora shakes her head. "He'll resurface when he's ready. I know he is inconsolable about letting his dark side out. It isn't easy letting the world see the monster you once were and hoped to never be again."

"Professor Harlow has no problem with that," I mumble.

Flora raises an eyebrow. "No, I'm afraid she doesn't. Hence her living assignment in the dungeon until further notice."

"I can't believe you let Jocelyn go," Jax complains. "She practically let Harlow kill Gilly!"

"Jocelyn is a troubled girl," Flora agrees, "but she has assured me she was not aware of her sister's actual doings with Alva." We start to protest, but Flora cuts us off. "Until I know otherwise, it is my job to believe her. She will stay here as a student—under my watchful eye, of course."

I'm not sure that's smart, but we have bigger problems than Jocelyn. No one knows when Alva will strike again or what she has planned next. Jax hasn't been able to find out anything from his father. He's made us swear not to blow his cover with

Flora. For now, we have to keep some secrets of our own. I'm sure the former Wicked Stepmother is doing the same.

"My job is to watch over all of my students, including you, Kayla." Flora puts a hand on Kayla's shoulder. "I know all about your deal with Rumpelstiltskin, and I promise that together we will find a way to lift the spell on your family."

Kayla tears up. "Thank you."

"So what's our next move?" I ask.

"*Your* next move is to go back to being students," Flora says. "Take a day off from all these dark doings and have fun."

Fun? We look at her like she's grown three heads.

"Miri, tell them what I have planned," Flora says.

Miri's brass mirror begins to glow. "There's a picnic lunch set up in the garden and a game of dodgeball waiting to be had in the courtyard, which has just been cleared of debris. And I'm told the ice cream is melting, so you don't want to wait too long to get out there."

"I'm up for that!" Ollie cheers.

"Good! Now go before I change my mind and have you write a paper!" Flora jokes. I never thought I'd see the day. "Oh, but first, I have something for Gillian." She pulls a note with a royal seal out of her desk drawer. We gather around to read it.

Miss Gillian Cobbler, thank you for your help once again in keeping evil at bay. Flora has told us of your father's shoemaking woes. Because of that, we would like to commission all glass slippers for the royal palace from his shop from now on.

—Princess Ella

"Wow. Does that mean someone in the royal family is actually nice?" Jax says, feigning shock as he shifts from one crutch to the other. "Who would have thought that would happen?"

I give him a look. "Thanks," I say, blushing as I look at our headmistress. "I'm sorry for calling you a stepmonster. And for, you know, thinking you were a villain again. I still have a lot of questions though."

Flora looks mildly amused. "Apology accepted, and I promise to answer more of your questions when your professors are back. You know, Gillian, villains *think* they have power, but the mistake they always make is the same—they have no idea how to use it." She scratches her chin. "True power is learning how to put others first and not judge a book by its cover, so to speak. I think you're doing a good job of that here at FTRS." She pauses. "But you still have a way to go before your stay is up."

"That's okay," I say. "I don't mind it here anymore."

Miri's mirror starts to glow again. "Flora? Call from the castle. Are you free to talk to Rapunzel?"

"Yes, please put her on hold, Miri." Flora points to the door. "Now all of you go and let me worry about villains for the rest of the day."

I watch Miri's mirror glow green, then purple, and I close the door.

"Ice cream?" Ollie asks.

"From curses and villains to ice cream," Maxine says as her eye droops. "Kind of a boring afternoon, don't you think?"

We walk toward the doors leading outside. When Ollie opens them, I bask in the warm sunlight on my face and the sound of laughter in the meadow. Balloons and bright pink tablecloths on the tables blow in the wind. As far as the eye can see, trolls, gnomes, fairies, ogres, and even the mer-folk have come up to sit on rocks at the lake nearby. It's nice to see everyone in a good mood.

They're happy.

At reform school.

Who would have guessed it?

I look to the right of the castle and see the crumbling exterior walls of the ballroom that are being redone. "I could use boring right now."

"Me too," says Kayla. For a moment, her wings appear, battered but resilient, and then they're gone again. I know it won't be long before they reappear. Or I want to snag something we could use in battle. Or Jax and Ollie sweet-talk their way into some intel we could use. The Hollow Woods lie in the distance, looking ominous and full of secrets that Maxine can't wait to uncover. Like where Alva is hiding. And how desperately a trapped Harlow wants to help her.

But those are all questions for another day.

"Dudes, come on! They've got vanilla and chocolate!" Ollie has reached the ice cream table and is already dishing it out. The ice cream oozes over the sides of the cups onto the table.

"Let's go be bored together," I say, squeezing Jax tight as we head for the melted ice cream and an afternoon bound to give us the best kind of bellyache.

Who's Who in Enchantasia

Headmistress Flora: Remember that whole glass slipper business with Cinderella? Flora is Princess Ella's formerly wicked stepmother. Now she runs Fairy Tale Reform School.

Professor Wolfington: Little Red Riding Hood has nothing to fear from this former big bad wolf. The only howling he does these days is when a student gets good grades in his history class at FTRS.

Madame Cleo: She made the Little Mermaid's life under the sea miserable, but these days the classy mermaid with the killer hair teaches charm classes and dance at FTRS. She's also got a bit of a short-term memory problem, which means detention is sometimes forgotten about!

Professor Harlow: Snow White's Evil Queen is still, well, kind of mean, but she means well now that she teaches FTRS students psychology and how to deal with their feelings.

Gottie: Remember the baddie who stuck Rapunzel in that tower? She's still bad, still on the loose, and she's looking for revenge on the princesses and kingdom of Enchantasia. Shiver!

Alva: Sleeping Beauty's dreamcaster could be alive or she could be dead. No one's seen her in years and they're glad. She's the scariest fairy villain in the kingdom.

Acknowledgments

Aubrey Poole, if I had a crown, I'd make you Queen of Enchantasia for all the work you put into this project! Thank you for helping me craft a richer story for our plucky heroine than I could ever imagine. I'm so lucky to be working with you and the whole team at Sourcebooks, including Adrienne Krogh, Kelly Lawler, Kate Prosswimmer, and designer Mike Heath, who gave me such a beautiful cover.

There wouldn't be an FTRS without Laura Dail, who found our fairy tale a wonderful home. Tamar Rydzinski, thanks for introducing FTRS to the world!

To Dan Mandel, the future is bright because of you! Extra special thanks also goes to Julia DeVillers (from here on out known as my fairy godmother), Elizabeth Eulberg, Leslie

Margolis, Sarah Mlynowski, Kieran Scott, and Jennifer E. Smith for all the feedback on my first middle grade project. A high five to Tyler's friend Gilly Miller for lending me her name for this book. (And for letting me borrow your mom, Marcy, who is the most voracious reader I know. Thanks for all the advice!)

Finally to my family, Mike, Tyler, Dylan, and even our Chihuahua, Captain Jack Sparrow—I couldn't do what I do without you guys. Thanks for being my rock. An extra-special shout-out to Ty for all the suggestions with the gargoyle scene. It's my favorite in the book and it's all because of you.

The adventure continues Spring 2016 with

CHARMED

Read on for a sneak peek!

CHAPTER 1

Charm School

Miri's voice crackles through the magic mirrors in Fairy Tale Reform School. "Let the first annual Wand What You Want hour begin!"

The warm sun is shining bright high above the castle walls, making me wistful for adventure. I can never sit still for long. I'm sure an actual spell would work better, but since I don't know one, I just imagine myself flying and—*bam!* I'm slowly floating up, up, up in the air. *Score!*

A Pegasus flies by me pulling a coach with four students in it.

"*Hi, Gilly!*" they shout and wave.

When you save your school from a wicked fairy,

people tend to remember your name. Even if you don't remember theirs.

"Hi!" I say, lying back like I'm floating on a cloud. *Wow, this is relaxing.* I stretch my arms wide and—*oops!*

My wand falls from my grasp. *Uh-oh.* I begin to plummet, spinning faster and faster with no sign of stopping. Before I can even think of a way to break my fall, *whoosh!* I feel my body hit a blanket and bounce up, then land again on a magic carpet.

"Ten minutes into Wand What You Want, and you're already having a near-death experience?" my friend Jax asks. His curly blond hair looks white in the bright sunlight. He casually waves his own wand in my direction with a glint in his violet eyes. "You're getting sloppy."

"I'm not getting sloppy!" I'm seriously offended by that statement. "How'd you even know where to find me?"

"I thought to myself, 'What would Gilly do with wand access for an hour?' and I knew right away you'd try to sneak home for a bit," Jax says. "Let's give it a go, shall we?"

My usual partner in crime steers our magic carpet over the castle walls and across the vast school grounds. Below I can see students fanned out on castle rooftops, in the garden mazes, and near the lake, all casting away with various results. Jax flies the carpet faster, the wind whipping our hair and making it hard to see. I push the hair away from my eyes and strain to see home.

There beyond the silver turrets of Royal Manor, where the princesses who rule our kingdom live, is my small village of Enchantasia. Somewhere down there, my family is working, playing, and hopefully missing me as much as I miss them. The carpet is nearing the Hollow Woods—which separates us and the village—and I lean forward. It's going to happen. We're going to leave school and see them! Closer we fly to the treetops...closer to the forest filled with ogres...closer to leaving school grounds when—*CRACKLE!*

Our magic carpet is suddenly stunned by an invisible wall that keeps us from escaping the school grounds. A magical scroll drops from the sky into our laps. "Leaving school grounds is forbidden!" it says in sparkling script that glows red like a warning. "Please return to the castle at once!" It's signed "Headmistress Flora."

"Smooth, Flora," Jax says. "Putting a barricade in the sky during wand training was clever."

"Leaving was a long shot, but maybe I could wave my wand and at least see what my family is up to," I say and gasp. "My wand! I need to go get it."

"Lose something, Gilly?" Our friend Maxine pilots a small flying swan boat I recognize from the Mother Goose carnival that was at school this past weekend. How does Maxine have one of those boats? Hmm… Bigger question: What's she doing in midair? Ogres don't usually like to be off the ground.

Maxine's right eye spins in its socket as she makes her way toward us with a crooked smile. Her thick neck is covered in layers of necklaces and the jewels she used to like to steal. (That's how she got thrown in FTRS. My offense was pick-pocketing and shoplifting.) Maxine tosses the wand toward me but it's snatched away.

"Come and get it!" Jax's roommate, Ollie, shouts. He's flying on the back of a black baby dragon, which does not seem smart. Ollie dives back toward the courtyard and Jax, Maxine, and I follow, landing seconds later in the courtyard I left only minutes before. I jump off the carpet and grab my wand from Ollie before his baby dragon can eat it. But I don't need to worry because—*poof!*—the dragon disappears.

"A baby dragon on school grounds?" My roommate, Kayla, waves her wand in the air dangerously, and I worry about what she could zap next. Her wings pop out of her back and she flutters to Ollie's side. As a fairy, Kayla can shrink to the size of a teacup, but at the moment, she towers over Ollie, white blond hair whipping in the wind. "That thing could burn down the whole school."

"We've already had that almost happen," Jax jokes. "Let's not do it again."

"Fine," Ollie says dejectedly. "I really wanted a pet." His eyes light up. "Snack break!" He waves his wand at the ground and conjures up an apple pie as big as the magic carpet I was just on. *Poof!* He also creates a supersize ice cream sundae and a plate of cookies as big as Maxine. He waves the wand again and a picnic basket, blanket, and plates appear on the grass beside it. "Let's eat!"

"We could use some ambiance," says Kayla who quickly transforms a dead rosebush into a beautiful plant with eye-popping roses in shades of fuchsia, electric blue, and lime green. Kayla flutters over to the blanket to help Ollie dish out dessert. He's using his wand as a cake knife and slicing pieces as big as my arm.

"Don't forget the music," says Maxine. She waves her wand in the air, and a flock of birds appears on a tree above us. They begin to chirp and hum in harmony. "*Yes!* It worked!" Maxine trudges over to the blanket happily, her ogre feet leaving deep footprints in the grass.

"Flora must have lost her mind to let a bunch of reform-school kids use wands for an hour," Jax says, flashing me a smile so blinding that I wish I had shades.

Poof! I use my wand to conjure up a pair. *Sweet!* I wish we could use wands every day instead of just in How a Wand Works 101. Madame Camille, our uptight fairy teacher, never lets us sign them out for homework, and every time someone screws up by zapping off their pinkie or growing their nose to three times its size, she says, "This is why Enchantasia doesn't allow wands 'til you're twenty-one!"

If I'd had a wand when I lived in the village, I wouldn't have had to steal food to help feed my brothers and sisters in our overcrowded boot. I could have just conjured up the finest treats Gnome-olia Bakery had to offer with a flick of my wrist. Then I wouldn't have been sentenced to Fairy Tale Reform School.

"Look, I get Flora disappearing to help Professor

Wolfington suppress his wolf side again, but where has she been since he came back?" Jax continues. "We never see her around school, and now she's letting us take wands out for a spin? Something's up."

"I'm with Jax," Maxine says, apple oozing down her chin as she chews. "My mini magical scroll has been showing me weird messages like 'She'll reappear when you're all distracted' instead of articles from *Happily Ever After Scrolls*."

Ollie gives me a look. Maxine swears her mini magical scroll is sending her messages, but mini magical scrolls only report the daily Enchantasia news. She seems to think her scroll is magical. Okay, *more* magical.

"Yesterday it said, 'Prepare. She is coming soon.'" Maxine cuts another slice of pie for herself that is as big as her head. "Who is coming? Flora? I quickly hid my scroll since I was supposed to be doing homework."

"I think Flora is just trying to give us some freedom," I say. "If they don't give us freedom every now and then, how are they going to see whether we're reforming?"

"Yeah, Maxine. Can't you just be happy we have an afternoon off from Villain to Hero: How to Make the Switch?" Kayla asks.

Maxine frowns. "I actually kind of miss Dragon Slaying 101, but sometimes learning about a dragon's weak spots is enough to make me want to breathe fire."

I sit up. "That gives me an idea." I begin to aim my wand but Jax stops me.

"I'm serious, guys," Jax says quietly. "Alva's on the loose, someone is spilling royal secrets, and Flora keeps disappearing. Don't you want to know what's going on?"

Jax is an undercover royal at a reform school. Of course he wants to sort things out and go back to being all royally. (He is secretly Rapunzel's brother, not that she knows that. She thinks he's off at boarding school, and Jax's dad had the royal court's memories bewitched so no one recognizes him.) And yes, I want to go home to my family, but in the past two months I've saved royals, kept our school from burning down, and had T-shirts made with my name on them. I need a short recess to relax.

"Can't we take an hour off from being good guys and enjoy doing something a bit wicked?" I conjure up Jax's favorite pie—figgy pudding—and his eyes go wide. "Let's eat before we plot!"

My friends and I begin slicing up the desserts in front of us when *poof!* They disappear right in front of our eyes.

"*Hey!*" Ollie's fork hangs in the air over a now-empty plate. "Who did that?"

I look around the courtyard. Through the stained glass windows inside the school, I can see flashes of light every time a wand is used. Some hallways are filled with water where mermaids swim with ease and students have transformed into sharks and octopuses. Other windows show students dressed like princesses and pirates, while another set of windows shows mischief that could get those kids detention for a week with Madame Cleo. But I couldn't see a single person pointing a wand our way.

Then I hear a sinister laugh. I exhale sharply and look closer at my surroundings. I point my wand directly at the black gargoyle statue near the courtyard door that I don't remember seeing earlier. The statue starts to spark and then it transforms into a girl with long, dark hair in a black dress covered with stars and moons.

"Ouch! That hurt!" Jocelyn rubs her butt, which has a burn mark on one of the half-moons. "You singed my dress!"

"You stole our dessert." I wave my wand, wondering what I could do to Jocelyn next. Turn her into a toad? Make her wear a pink princess dress since she's allergic to any color but black? Put duct tape over her mouth so she can't cast any other spells?

"Sorry for the interruption, students," Miri's voice is back over the magical loudspeaker system. "Headmistress Flora would like me to remind you that illegal use of magic—such as escape attempts, turning your roommate into a toad, or using wand work for monetary gain—is not allowed. Today's Wand What You Want experiment is to see how you handle having a bit of wand freedom. Remember that. Thank you!"

Fiddlesticks.

"Did you want to join us?" Maxine asks awkwardly. She may be slightly afraid of the Evil Queen's little sister, but I'm not. Professor Harlow is now tucked away in the FTRS dungeons. Why Headmistress Flora allowed Jocelyn to stay in school is beyond me.

"She's not welcome here," I say calmly. "Give our food back."

Jocelyn shrugs. "Make me."

I use my wand to make the food reappear.

Jocelyn zaps it and makes it disappear.

I bring the food back.

Jocelyn makes it vanish.

Appear, disappear, appear, disappear.

Finally I snap. With my wand high above my head, I lift Ollie's giant apple pie and let the whole thing drop on Jocelyn's head. She screams. "Score!" I shout.

"Gilly, don't start with her," Kayla says, growing nervous. She's still a bit jittery around villains. I can't say I blame her. She was blackmailed by Alva for years, forced to help the evil fairy in exchange for information on the whereabouts of her missing family. (Who are now trees. It's complicated.)

"I'm fine!" I say, but while I'm laughing, Jocelyn is conjuring. *Smack!* A piece of pudding pie flies into my face.

"How does the pudding taste, Cobbler?" Jocelyn taunts. "I bet you guys could never afford pudding in your boot."

"We can now, while you're an orphan with an evil sister in lockup." I shoot a cherry pie at her face. It explodes and covers her with cherries. *Hee.* I look to Kayla for approval, but that "orphan" comment leaves her cold. Okay, maybe that was a bit harsh. I'm so busy staring at Kayla that I don't feel the crackle 'til it's too late.

"My hair!" I screech as my head begins to glow for a

second, then stops. I feel my hair. It's all still there. I exhale. "Ha! Your spell didn't work!" I sing out.

"Um, Gilly?" Ollie asks. "Did you always have a purple streak in your hair?"

I pull the front of my hair forward and gasp. A deep purple stripe is now running through my long, brown hair. Jocelyn bursts out laughing.

"Change it back!"

Jocelyn shrugs. "Can't. I didn't spell you. I cursed you. It can't be undone."

"Why you…" *Zap!* I send a vat of chocolate ice cream raining down on her head.

"Enough!" Ollie says as a wall of dead fish smacks him in the face, leaving a slimy trail on his mocha-colored skin.

"You can't do that." Jax sounds funny holding his nose. He quickly conjures up a massive bowl of cooked spinach, which hits Jocelyn with a loud *splat*.

Soon food is flying through the air like hail. Broccoli is raining from the rooftop. Mashed potatoes create walls we can use as barricades. Radishes hit Kayla in the head and give her welts. We're so busy conjuring up food that we don't hear the sound at first.

KABOOM!

The noise and the low rumble that follows are enough to make us all jump.

Kayla wipes stew from her hair. "What was that?" She sounds worked up.

Jocelyn spits out cherry pits that have appeared in her mouth. "Don't get your wings twisted. I'm sure Professor Biggins just misfired a potion he was working on."

"If there was a reason to panic, the alarms would have gone off." I listen carefully.

KABOOM!

This time the sound is so loud that we grab each other to keep from falling.

WOO-OOH! WOO-OOH!

The school security system is going off. Seconds later, our wands disappear along with the picnic, magic carpet, and my comfy clothes. My dreaded uniform is back, but that's not my biggest concern. I know what we're all thinking: the last time the alarm tripped was when we had a break-in from Alva.

"I'm going," I say and head toward the courtyard door.

"So am I." Jocelyn tries to beat me to the doorway. We each try to push the other out of the way.

I push her back. "You just want the distraction to help your sister escape the dungeons. I'm not going to let you help her!"

"Try to stop me!" Jocelyn pushes me so hard that I fall. I quickly jump up and follow her into the hallway. It's chaos. Students are running in every direction, but I follow Jocelyn's food-splattered dress. I can hear my friends calling me, but I don't stop.

"Students, this is Headmistress Flora speaking." I hear Cinderella's formerly wicked stepmother's voice ring out from the castle's mirrors. "Please remain in your dorm rooms. There is a situation, but we have it under control. There is no cause for alarm."

A hallway switches in front of me, but I dive through it and land right on top of Jocelyn. We're somehow outside again—the new hallway leads us to the school lake.

KABOOM!

"Ouch!" Jocelyn yells as my friends fly out of yet another hallway, dropping onto the same grassy patch near the lake.

"Holy shipwreck!" Ollie says, pointing to something in the distance on the water. I hear a commotion and shouting. "Duck!"

We drop to the ground just in time to see a cannonball whiz past our heads.

"Um, guys?" Kayla's frown deepens. "What's a pirate ship doing in the *lake* at Fairy Tale Reform School?"

About the Author

Jen Calonita is the author of the Secrets of My Hollywood Life series and other books like *Sleepaway Girls* and *Summer State of Mind*, but Fairy Tale Reform School is her first middle grade series. She rules Long Island, New York, with her husband Mike, princes Tyler and Dylan, and Chihuahua Captain Jack Sparrow, but the only castle she'd ever want to live in is Cinderella's at Walt Disney World. She'd love for you to drop her a line at jencalonitaonline.com or keep the fairy tale going at happilyeverafterscrolls.net.